Keeping Busy

A Novella

Tracy Gray

ISBN-13-9798696515809

Cover Design: Kerry Sovde Design
Editing: LRB1 Style! Editing Services

Printed in the United States of America

Dedication

This book is for those in my inner circle who always answer "the call" – most specifically LaShann Rochelle Bailey (who answers the call **REPEATEDLY** and with a dedication that sometimes I even have trouble matching).

Kacie Gray-Caruthers (who is forced to answer the call, but does it graciously…every time).

Jacqualyne "Jackie" Nichols (who is never too busy no matter what time the "call" comes in, and ALWAYS makes herself available for me).

Brandy Means (who makes sure to always cheer me on).

Shwanda Cross (who volunteered to answer the call).

Kerry Sovde (who was dragged into answering the call, but who has become an integral part of this book journey.

Thank you, ladies! Because of you being you, I can be and do me.

~ *Tracy Gray*

Table of Content

Title Page   1

Copyright   2

Dedication   3

Chapter 1   5

Chapter 2   20

Chapter 3   37

Chapter 4   52

Chapter 5   61

Chapter 6   82

Chapter 7   99

Chapter 8   113

Chapter 9   125

Chapter 10   144

Chapter 11   159

The End   169

Afterword   170

Maddox

<u>1</u>

How the hell did my life get here? I whispered to myself, looking up at the ornate cathedral ceiling. I thought about the last few months, and shook my head. The truth was that I only had myself to blame. I was the one who latched onto Ainsley, even though I knew that she didn't have a damn thing going for herself and was only with me because I'm Maddox Mayhew. I was the one who repeatedly made bad decisions where she was concerned. I was the one who was out of control on June 21st - the one who drank until I passed out and didn't hear the shit that was happening right under my nose.

Of course I never expected Ainsley to be my downfall, she was just something to do for a minute. I never expected her to have another dude in my house. I never expected them to be getting high, and having sex in my house. And I definitely didn't expect her to blame me, when he flipped out and beat her ass in my house. Then I was arrested in my own house, removed from my own house, and charged with assault and battery from an event that took place in my own house.

If it hadn't been for the cameras from the extensive security system I'd installed capturing the whole shit and vindicating me, I would have lost everything. My career. My livelihood. My future. My reputation. My name.

As it was, I still took a hit. While it took mere hours for the story about me being arrested and held for assault and battery against Ainsley Neuberg to hit the media, it took two days for my team to get my security footage to Ainsley's team, and even longer for her to recant the story and clear my name. Normally, the media isn't even pressed about what football players are into during the off-season, but leave it to me and my fuck ups to draw all kinds of unwanted attention. Especially the attention that I caught from several women's groups calling for the Leopards to release me, and seriously threatening my endorsement deals.

It didn't help my cause at all, that even after she recanted her lie, Ainsley went on every talk show, podcast, blog or vlog that would have her. She accused me of having been abusive during our entire time together. Not physically abusive, needless to say, but mentally emotionally and verbally abusive, which of course drove her to take drugs and sleep with other men. I had to threaten to take legal action against her to get her crazy, attention-seeking ass to stand down. It was a shit show.

And while her stories were obviously untrue, I still felt like the consensus was, "***that's what I got for messing around with a white chick. A black man should know better.***" My reputation was in the toilet, and I was coming into my last season under the current contract, not turning shit around and quickly didn't bode well for my prospects as an unrestricted free-agent. The only thing that I had going for me was the numbers I posted last season. All good. Voted back to the Pro-Bowl for the seventh time, nominated for the Art Rooney Award - I had a good season. But the shenanigans with Ainsley did take a toll.

Luckily, my professional team was loyal. My agent, Ayana Truesdale, who I referred to as "True" was definitely loyal to me, even though she was disappointed in me for "taking up with Ainsley's ass" in the first place. My attorney, Brandon, was loyal, but he didn't have a choice, since 1; he's my younger brother and 2; I paid for him to get the law degree. And finally, my sports management team stuck with me. Sydnie Whitmore was my rep, and she knew her shit. Things were going to turn around for me, I just had to figure out how to be patient while they did.

At the moment, I was sitting in church. I planned to be patient, but a little divine intervention never hurt. It wasn't Sunday morning or anything. Actually, it was a Tuesday afternoon and I was sitting in a pew at St. Phillip Neri Catholic church on the South Side of Chicago. It wasn't my "home" church, but I had grown up a few blocks away. I was actually raised at (read: forced to attend by my grandmother) Fellowship Baptist Church, but when my grandmother needed a hit of Jesus during the mid-week, she wasn't too proud to walk down to the local Catholic church and say her prayers, believing that we had different ways of doing so, but we all served the same Jesus.

"Lord," I began the prayer, having no idea where it would end up, "I know I've been doing things the "Maddox" way and fuck...messing them up. But I want to try to walk with you, Man. I just need you to show me that you're walking with me. Amen." I crossed myself in the name of the father, the son, and the Holy Spirit, having no idea why I was doing it, except that was what my grandmother had always done, then stood up. I walked over to where they kept the candles, placed a few bills in the donation box, then lit a candle for my grandmother (God rest her soul), one for the homeless, and one for the helpless, then I headed back to my grandmother's house. True was flying into Chicago to meet with me, and she was bringing Sydnie Whitmore with her. It was time to take action.

Sydnie Whitmore was impressive as hell. As far as I was concerned, it would be hard for me to do better. She double majored at Walker University, earning degrees in both Economics and Communication & Media. She was educated, highly skilled and had mastered the art of the "spin."

"Look, Maddox." She said to me, her serious brown eyes piercing mine. "Let's be real. It's not just the clusterfuck that happened on your premises the night of June 21st that has affected your reputation and cachet. It was the bar brawl that…"

"That wasn't a brawl." I muttered.

"Stop being an asshole and listen to her Maddox. You pulled both of us away from sunny California to finish cleaning up your shit before training camp. Stop being an asshole." True chastised.

"It's sunny here, too, True." I couldn't help pointing out, just to mess with her.

She ignored me. Well, actually she rolled her eyes up to the ceiling, but then she ignored me.

Technically, True worked for me, but if you viewed our dynamic, it would be hard to tell. True was a mother figure in my life. She treated me, and talked to me the same way she talked to her own son, who was also in the league and was one of my closest dudes. She fought for me, like she fought for him, too. Pulled my coat-tail, and praised me the same, as well. She was a mama bear and a pit bull in a skirt. I hired her on draft day. There was never a doubt in my mind that she would be my agent. She was willing to and capable of moving mountains for her clients.

I turned my gaze back to Sydnie. She was a pretty girl. Skin the color of dark chocolate, creamy and smooth. She wore her naturally curly hair wild and loose in a huge afro. Her eyes were dark brown, and intelligent. She didn't miss much.

"What were you saying?" I asked her.

"What has affected your reputation was the bar brawl that happened, allegedly because a patron got a little too friendly with Ainsley Neuberg. Then there was the car accident, and the rumors about you being drunk when it happened...with Ainsley in the truck. Then there was the time that you climbed into Buckingham Fountain with her to…"

"Which was the dumbest shit ever." True cut in. "How are you gonna disrespect your hometown like that, Busy?"

She called me by my childhood nickname, but that didn't really soften the blow. "Come on, True. You know I would never disrespect Chicago like that. I wasn't trying to climb into Buckingham Fountain. Who the fuck tries to climb into Buckingham Fountain?"

"I don't know. But your ass was in there. With...her."

Nobody hated Ainsley Neuberg more than Ayana Truesdale. If Ainsley ever ended up missing, I would already know who to suspect.

"I was trying to get her dumb ass out." I defended myself.

"Maybe if you weren't drunk, you would've known that getting in there yourself was dumb as hell." She eyed me meanly, but I knew it was all love. "Do I need to find a 12 step program for you, Busy? Tell me now, while we're in the off season, and still have a few weeks before training camp."

"I'm good." I assured her. "I'm not drinking. I don't even wanna think about drinking."

She softened her glare. "Look, I know this is about your grandmother, I know it is. Her death has been...devastating for every member of your family."

I wanted to tune her out, because the last thing I wanted to do was talk about my grandmother, but I didn't. I needed to man-up and stop wallowing in my self-pity.

"But she put more into you, than for you to fall apart when you need to hold it together the most. You're 32 years old, Busy. You've got what? Four, maybe five years left in this league. Finish out on a high note, Baby. Let's get this money, and make sure you have

9

enough to retire and live comfortably on. Let's repair your image, so that you can put on one of those expensive ass suits that you love to buy, and sit in front of the camera talking about football, instead of being out there on the field punishing your body playing it. Okay?"

I nodded my head in the affirmative. "Okay."

We both looked at Sydnie.

"Okay." She said. "Here's what we're doing to repair your image."

Sydn e went through a list, which included me being highly visible for the last week of the youth camp that I sponsored in Chicago each summer. She talked about her plans to have me do a few PSAs about violence against women, and make a donation to a women's shelter. I was definitely with that. We talked about the upcoming charity event for violence against women that I was expected to chair, and about me being the face of a campaign for "black and missing" women and children.

"That brings me to my next point, Maddox." Sydnie told me. "I would like to see you 'settle down'."

There were air quotes used around the phrase "settle down."

"In what way?"

"I think it would be good if we brought in a woman that could appear strategically on your arm at events, and in the media. You know, someone…"

"Black?" True asked.

"I was gonna say high profile." I commented.

Sydnie was slow to speak. "Black would be great. Since you were voted *Football Life's* Sexiest Defensive Player two years ago, women have loved you. Black women in particular. They're some of your biggest supporters and fans, Maddox. You're a good-looking single guy that they can fantasize about, but polling shows that as a group they won't support you if they feel that you don't support them. i.e.: dating outside of your race. Shenanigans with women who are...outside of your race are completely frowned upon."

"They didn't need a poll for that." True said. "Any black woman will tell you, getting in all of this legal trouble behind some white woman and her foolishness makes us feel like…"

"I got what I deserved. I know." And I did know. How many times had my grandmother ridden my ass about staying the hell away from white women and their foolishness? Truth be told, white women weren't even my preference. Still, when Ainsley approached me at that party, I entertained her, instead of blowing her off.

"So," Sydnie continued. "This woman would just be there to, you know, show the world that you're a good guy - a good 'partner', if you will. She'll smile, and look at you adoringly. You'll hold on to her arm when you two walk, open car doors for her. You know? Just basically take control of the narrative of who you are as a person off the field, instead of letting Ainsley control it. She has a five day head-start, but unless she can produce some video or other receipts to back up her claims, I think she's running out of steam."

"Unless you got her pregnant. Is there any chance that you got her pregnant, Busy?" True eyed me.

"Nah. I mean, she was smashing dude in my house, she could be pregnant. Who the hell knows? And she could pretend that it's mine, and drag this thing out for 9 months, but once the baby comes, it won't be mine."

"We'll deal with that if it comes up." Sydnie said, typing furiously into her phone. "But for now, is there any woman that you know who would be willing to help you out in this capacity? She doesn't need to have celebrity status, you have your own celebrity, Maddox. You're a household name. I think the most important thing, is that the candidate be believable. She needs to be pretty, and sophisticated, and..."

"Level-headed." That was True. "We don't need any hot heads making the situation worse than it already is."

"True." Sydnie agreed, "and if she could have a good background - nothing in her past that could embarrass or ignite another firestorm, that would be fabulous."

"How long are we talking?" True asked.

Sydnie looked up from her phone. "I'm thinking, at least through the season. Could be longer. I feel most comfortable saying let's play it by ear."

"I don't have anybody off the top of my head." I said, slowly. I mean, of course I knew women. Plenty of them. And I knew women who would certainly be down for pretending to be my lady for an indefinite amount of time, but it would take time to weed through the contenders. I wasn't interested in rushing into this situation with just anybody. "Let me think about it."

"Don't think too long, Maddox. I would like to see you have things in place in time for Jennifer Zuriela's charity event."

"This Friday?" I asked.

"It would be great if this young lady was your date to that. We need to get a lot of mileage out of this before you head into training camp. Then we'll pick back up again when you get out."

"Basically, you need to have somebody by tomorrow, at the latest." True eyed me. "That's not a lot of time if we have to - provide somebody."

I chuckled at her choice of words. "You mean make some kind of 'mutually beneficial' arrangement, True? Yeah. Nah, I can't give you a name or anything at the moment, but I would prefer not to have to use a 'professional'."

"Why you gotta say it like that? I'm not gonna hire you no prostitute."

"I know." I assured her. "Because we won't be hiring anybody. I have friends. I can make this happen."

"Well, in the interim, can you have Brandon contact me?" Sydnie asked. "We'll need to draw up a contract, because regardless if this person is a friend or a professional, we need to make sure that she signs an NDA. We don't need any surprises when she decides to write a tell-all book five years from now."

"Got ya." I agreed easily.

Later that evening, the doorbell rang at my grandmother's house. I wasn't expecting anybody, as True and Sydnie were long gone. My security guy, Heavy, was out south with his family during his time off, so I was alone in the spot. I normally didn't have trouble when I was at home, but as of late, Chicago had been a little unpredictable, so I needed to be smart. I walked over to the window, and moved the drapes, so that I could see the front porch. Standing there, as petite and as fragile as ever, but holding a huge wooden tray that looked heavy as hell, was my grandmother's 72-year-old former neighbor.

I moved to the door quickly, swinging it, and the screen door open - taking the tray from Bonita Watson-Granville's hands.

"Why thank you, Busy. Always were such a gentleman." She stated, following me into the house that had been her second home for all of the years she had been neighbors with my grandmother.

"You're welcome, Miss Bo. What brings you over here?" I took the tray into the kitchen, and set it down on the granite island that I'd had installed when I updated my grandmother's kitchen several years earlier.

"Well, I knew you were over here, and I figured you hadn't eaten, so I brought you dinner."

As soon as she said that, I noticed the scents wafting from the tray I was just carrying.

"How'd you know I was here?" I asked, lifting the cloche from the platter to reveal fried chicken, mashed potatoes, asparagus spears, and a gravy boat filled with the smooth, creamy brown liquid.

"Boy, I'm an old lady. I spend a lot of time looking outta my windows. I saw you last night when you pulled up in that fancy truck of yours."

I smiled, as I pulled her into a hug. "You're not old. You know you're a spring chicken, still got these men out here sniffing behind you."

She threw her head back with laughter as she took a seat at the island. "Get on with yourself, Boy. Only thing men my age can smell is Icy Hot and Ben Gay."

I eyed her. "You want me to introduce you to somebody? There's some guys on my team that would…"

"Leave me alone, Busy."

I chuckled as I walked over to the sink and washed my hands.

"Look at you. Vera would be so proud of you."

"I don't know about all that." I mumbled, as I took the platter of food from the tray and placed it in front of myself.

"Why do you think she wouldn't be proud? Because you made some missteps here lately? Believe me, she still would've been proud of you. You're such a good man, Busy. You've taken care of Brandon and Xavier. You look after this house. You run your sports camp. You donate your time and your money to things that are important. You care about people, Busy. That would make her proud."

I gave a half-hearted shrug as I bit into a piece of chicken. Nobody could fry chicken like Bonita Watson-Granville, not even my own beloved grandmother, and my grandmother could cook her ass off.

"Man, this is good, Miss Bo."

She chuckled. "My best friend was good at a lot of things, but she never did master the art of frying chicken." She teased.

I grinned, and took another bite.

"So, what's going on? Talk to me, Maddox."

I froze, the chicken stopping in mid-air on its way to my mouth. The only time my grandmother or Miss Bonita ever called me "Maddox" was when I was in trouble.

"About what?" I hedged, resuming my assault on the food in front of me.

"About what you plan to do about the scandal that little young heifer caused you. I saw Ayana Truesdale over here earlier, with some little black beauty of a girl. She gonna help you?"

"That's Sydnie Whitmore, my sports management rep. She's helping me get a handle on my public persona."

"Good. Good." She nodded her head. "Vera's been coming to me every night in my dreams."

I kept eating. I knew she would keep talking, so there was no reason for me to interject anything.

15

"She's worried about you."

Hell, I was worried about me, too. The stress of the situation, and the fact that my life started going to shit so close to the start of the season stayed on my mind.

"Why?" I fronted.

"You know why. What does that pretty little girl suggest you do to get your reputation fixed?"

I told her about Sydnie's suggestions ending with her idea that I needed to "settle down" for a while.

"She knows her stuff. So, which one of your young ladies are you going to bring off the bench?"

"Don't say it like that, Miss Bo." I couldn't help chuckling. "Like I've got women waiting around for the opportunity to spend time with me."

"Don't you, though?" Her tone was flat. "Haven't you had it like that since you were in high school? Oh, those little fast-tailed girls who wouldn't leave you alone used to drive Vera crazy."

"Yeah, I know." I agreed. If anybody knew how much they used to drive her crazy, it was me. I had to hear about it all the time. As if I had any control over their behavior. "Anyway, I haven't really had a chance to think about who I want to ask. It's kind of a big favor."

"To spend time with you, and pretend to enjoy it? Sounds like the easiest job in the world to me, Busy. If I was 50 years younger."

We both laughed.

"Well, don't think too long, Sweetheart. This heifer is out here dragging your reputation and good name through the mud. Vera worked too hard to keep you on the straight and narrow to let a no-good rapscallion like that one make you out to be somebody you aren't." She stood up, holding onto the island for support.

It bugged me to see Miss Bo getting older. I knew what happened as the years started to slide by - we lost our elders one by one. I had just lost my grandmother. I wasn't ready to think about losing Miss Bo.

"How long are you gonna be in town?" She shuffled over to the cabinet, pulled out a glass and made her way over to the refrigerator. She filled the glass, first with ice, then with water, and set it down within reach for me.

"Another week or so. I have to finish up my youth camp. It'll be over next Thursday, we'll do the awards on Friday, and that'll wrap it up. Then, I'm headed out. I gotta get my life in order before I head to training camp." I took a long swallow of the ice cold water. "Thank you."

She nodded. "I'm going to get back over here before you leave."

"You don't have to do that, Miss Bo. I don't want you standing up at the stove trying to cook for me."

"I like standing up at my stove, cooking. And since you aren't the boss of me, you can't tell me who to do it for."

I smirked at her. "You trying to air me out?"

"I just aired you out." She gave me a hug that communicated both her strength and her love for me. "I'm gonna see your grandmother tonight in my dreams. We're gonna figure this whole thing out."

I wanted to ask her how she was having all of these conversations with my deceased grandmother, but I let it rock. One thing I learned a long time ago was that the elders worked in their own mysterious ways.

Mecca

<u>2</u>

I watched my mother, Janaye Goode, strut into my office. That was my mother, she wasn't a walker. To get from one place to another, she either strutted, bopped, pranced, strolled, or breezed. Today, she strutted.

"Hey Ma." I said, looking up at her.

"Hey Baby." Gracefully, she slid into the chair opposite me. "How's it going?"

My mom and I owned *The Goode Experience Dance Academy*. For years, she owned it and I worked there as a dance instructor. Now that she was considering retirement one day, she let me buy in and we were business partners. On top of being an owner of the dance academy, I also choreographed on the side. Professional and collegiate dance teams frequently invited me in as a guest choreographer and asked me to prepare a routine or two for a season.

"It's going well." I had just finished counting the box office receipts from our summer production. "I've been organizing the receipts, so I can take them to Trevor." Trevor Wrightwood was our accountant.

"Then my timing is perfect. Aunt Bo called me this morning."

Auntie Bo was my mother's aunt, making her my great aunt. She was the matriarch of our family - my grandfather's eldest sister. Auntie Bo's husband died early on in their marriage before they'd had the opportunity to have children of their own, but she'd had a hand in raising every child from the Watson family tree, including my siblings, Cairo and British and me.

My parents were in the entertainment industry when they had us. My father is actually still in the entertainment industry. He's a world-renowned DJ, who's been doing music for almost 30 years. Not a DJ, as in "radio disc jockey," but an actual DJ with scratching and cutting and stuff. He started with turntables, and crates of vinyl records, making mixes and providing the turn-up for parties all over the world. He's most loved, admired and respected in the Hip Hop and House Music genres.

My mother started her career as a video dancer when girls still actually danced in videos. She was the "featured" girl in a lot of music videos in the 1990s and was invited to tour the world as a dancer with several different artists. As the industry started to change, she was able to parlay her accomplishments into a successful career as a choreographer. Later, she opened the dance academy, so she could stay home with us, while my dad continued to travel the world.

So, even though all of the Watson children had spent their fair share of time with Auntie Bo, when Cairo, British and I outgrew the novelty of constantly touring the world with our parents and were ready to stay in one place, we practically lived with her.

"She wants you to stop by her house today. Said she needs to talk to you." My mother told me.

"Okay. I'll stop by right after I drop these receipts off at Trevor's office.

Auntie Bo wore a smile on her pretty face when she greeted me at her front door later that morning.

"Get on in here, Pudding." She said, calling me by her own personal nickname for me and pulling me into a warm embrace.

I hugged her back with vehemence. She always gave the best hugs, the kind that left you feeling loved and cherished. "Hey Auntie. I heard you needed to talk to me."

"I do." She assured me. "Come on into the kitchen. We can have some of these tea cakes I made."

What she would call a "tea cake," I would call a cookie. So, I asked, "are they shortbread?" She knew I loved shortbread.

"Aren't those your favorite?" She replied, and instantaneously I understood that she was trying to butter me up for the ask. Whatever she wanted to talk to me about was going to require sacrifice on my part. She obviously didn't automatically expect me to accede to doing it.

"They sure are." I agreed following her into the kitchen.

I sat down at her island and waited. My great aunt wasn't the type of person that you could rush into anything, so I didn't even bother, even though I was dying to know why she called me to her home. I waited patiently while she placed three shortbread tea cakes on a saucer for me, then filled a mug with what I knew was homemade hot chocolate.

Finally, she sat down next to me. "Pudding, I need a favor."

"Okay." I said, slowly nodding my head. I hoped I could do whatever she was going to ask of me, because she was Auntie Bo. I loved her to pieces, and appreciated everything she had done for my siblings and me when we were children.

"Well, actually, Busy needs a favor, but he won't ask you and even if he did, you would probably say no. So, I'm asking you, because it needs to get done, and you need to be the one to do it."

First of all, what? I was lost.

"When you say 'Busy', are you talking about Busy, Busy? Maddox Mayhew, Busy? Busy from across the street?"

"How many children called Busy do you know?"

"You ain't gotta get sassy, Auntie Bo." I said with a smirk. "You were talking so fast, that I really didn't even know what you said."

"Busy needs you, Pudding."

I twisted up my face. "Needs me how? Because from as far back as I can remember, Busy has rarely said more than three words at a time to me."

"Doesn't matter." She shook her head. "He needs you now. And you need to be there for him."

"Be there for him how, Auntie? You're not answering any of my questions. And how can I be there for somebody who has known me since toddlerhood, and hasn't said more than 50 words total since then?"

21

Again, Auntie Bo wasn't one to be made to do anything. I knew that I could ask her 100 ways to Sunday what she was talking about, and she wasn't going to spill all of the tea until she was good and ready.

"Do you watch the news, Pudding?"

Okay, so now we were going to segue into talking about the news. Whatever.

"Sometimes." I took a bite of my tea cake and hummed happily. It was delicious.

"Have you seen the stuff that's been going on with Busy in his...personal life?"

Oooookkkkaaaaayyy. Now, I could admit that I didn't really watch the news. I got all of my news from the Yahoo home page, and Busy's dumb ass had been a thumbnail there for well over a week. I finally understood where she was coming from.

"Yeah, I have." I said, drinking hot chocolate and eating tea cakes with voracity, now. Whatever she wanted me to do for Busy, I was almost certain that it wasn't going to happen. Which was too bad, because I hated to disappoint my aunt.

"His sports management representative...I think that's what he called her."

"That sounds right." I said, chomping into my third tea cake.

"She wants to help him clean up his image, and one of her suggestions is that he make appearances with and be photographed with a nice young lady at important events, like this charity event situation he has coming up."

My delicious cookie turned to sawdust in my mouth.

For real, Auntie Bo? I wanted to ask, but I knew better.

"He knows tons of women. Tons of tons. I'm sure one of his ho...lady friends would be happy to help him. He doesn't need me. He wouldn't want me. As a matter of fact, does he even know you've got me over here trying to drag me into his business?"

"No, he doesn't." She admitted. "But that doesn't matter, because when I tell him that you're his girl, he won't give me any back talk...unlike you."

22

I laughed. "Auntie…"

"Pudding, this is serious. I know you aren't friends with Busy, and he's just the kid from across the street to you, but I love that boy. And I loved his grandmama, God rest her soul. He only has a few years left in the league, and I want him to end on a high note. He's been an upstanding example of black excellence throughout his career. All he did was pick the wrong heifer to run around with and now his reputation and good name are in jeopardy."

"Well, he did pick her." I shrugged my shoulders and swigged the last of my hot chocolate. "He kinda only has himself to blame."

"He lost his grandmama, Mecca Noelle Goode. She raised him since he was ten years old."

Shit. It was getting real. She used my whole name. Playtime was apparently over.

"Do you think you would have the capacity to be your best self and make airtight decisions if Janaye Goode dropped dead?"

If my mama dropped dead, I would be somewhere balled up, so I got her point. "You're right." I admitted.

"Show people the same grace and mercy that you would want them to show you." She scolded. "Now, as I was saying, he needs your help."

"Okay, on the strength of my love for you, I would probably help him. I mean, we kinda grew up together. We're certainly not friends, but we aren't enemies. But you don't understand what you're asking, Auntie. Maddox Mayhew is in the NFL, he's famous. His face is on billboards, in magazines, on television. His name is on gym shoes, on the back of jerseys. There are entire websites dedicated to being his fan. He probably has a gang of social media followers. Any girl that gets involved with him, even if it is just for appearances sake is going to be subjected to the skewering…the dragging from internet trolls. People are going to delve into my background, my past, my business and try to find

23

out things about me, about my family. Pictures and videos are going to show up on the internet. It's not like I can go to dinner with Busy, go home and just live. Look at the chick who lied on him, she's been the top story in the media for weeks now, and for what? I don't want that."

"You're the one, Mecca. The only one." She said softly.

Who the fuck was I? Neo from The Matrix? Why the hell was I the one? I looked into her face, and I had my answer.

I sighed heavily. "You been talking to dead people, again, Auntie?"

My Auntie Bo talked to more dead people than that little boy in the movie. I didn't understand how she got to have all these conversations with dead people, but I was glad that I didn't have that ability.

"I don't talk to dead people, they show me stuff in my dreams."

"And they showed you me?" I asked, before I thought better of it. Then I held up my hand. "Don't answer that. I don't want to know."

We sat there in silence for a few moments. Finally, I sighed again. "Auntie, have Maddox come over here. I'll talk to him about it. I'm not promising that I'm going to do it, but I'll at least promise to talk to him about it."

Damn! I thought to myself. This wasn't my best idea.

Maddox "Busy" Mayhew walked into my Auntie Bo's house looking like a more muscular, taller, sexier, more handsome, more panty-wetting version of the boy that used to ignore me growing up. I watched from the cut as he stepped into the foyer, and pulled my aunt into a hug.

"You and my grandma figured all of my problems out last night in your dreams?" He teased.

I shook my head and chuckled silently. My aunt wasn't ashamed to let anybody know that dead people felt perfectly comfortable coming to her and "chopping it up" in the middle of the night.

"Let's sit in the front room and talk. Come on, Pudding."

And that was when Maddox Mayhew noticed me. The easy smile that he had been wearing for my aunt faded from his countenance. His face registered several thoughts and emotions that I couldn't read, but when it landed on, "*oh, hell nah,*" I knew exactly what he was thinking.

"Miss Bo," he said, completely stopping his forward motion. "Please don't let this be what I think it is."

I wasn't quite sure whether to be offended or not, because the truth of the matter was that while I acted like Maddox never spoke more than 50 words to me, the same could be said about any of the Watson girls. Well, with the exception of my cousin Clarke Cross. He would talk to her, but Clarke had that "take no prisoners" personality. If she wanted you to talk to her, dammit, you were gonna talk to her. So, he did. But even she gave up after a few years and wrote Maddox off along with the rest of us. So, it wasn't personal against me, Maddox Mayhew wasn't checking for any of us.

"Well, I won't know what you think it is, until we sit down and talk about it." Auntie Bo reasoned.

The three of us sat down in her well-appointed living room, Auntie Bo and Maddox on the sofa, me in the wing chair facing them.

"Busy, my Pudding here, is your girl." She said simply.

He started to speak, but she held up one of her little bony hands, and he closed his mouth, just like his grandmother had taught him to do when an elder was speaking.

"I called my Pudding and asked her to come over here. When she arrived, I sprang this whole thing on her. I've asked her to do this for you, as a favor to me, because it's no secret, Maddox, how you have treated my grand nieces over the years. I have watched them be more than pleasant to you, while you in return have been nothing more than aloof, antisocial and detached towards them. They're all gorgeous, so for a while there, I was sure you were batting for the other team."

I couldn't help choking on a chuckle at his dismayed expression when she said that.

"But Vera assured me that you weren't. Then I spied you running around with the little fast-tailed girls in the neighborhood, and assumed that was what you liked. Since I knew my grand nieces weren't fast in the tail, I assumed that it was all for the best that you never took up with any of them. Anyway, we're here now, and we're gonna let the past be the past. Right, Pudding?"

She caught me off guard. I thought we were roasting Maddox's ass, how did I get pulled into the foray?

"I'll try. I'm still a little salty, though." I admitted.

"Saltiness aside. Nobody's gonna believe it if you show up with some little ugly, or homely girl, Busy...or a super polished professional. Pudding's perfect. She's beautiful, classy, smart, and urbane. She's the entire package."

While I appreciated my aunt's praise, it did start to rub me the wrong way - kind of like she was pouring it on. "You don't have to sell me to him, Auntie." I said, beating back the attitude that wanted to sneak into my tone. "You might want to start selling him to me." I muttered.

But not softly enough, because she heard me.

"I'm not selling either of you all to anybody. Busy is going to do this, because this is his best option for success, and he's a businessman at heart, so he understands that. You're going to do it, as a favor to your favorite aunt." She watched both of us for any sign of defiance. "I think you two need to spend some time talking to each other and getting to know one another. Nobody is going to believe you're sweethearts if you can't find a way to bridge this…"

"Awkwardness?" I supplied.

She rolled her eyes at me. "You need to figure out a way to like each other. It'll make the ruse that much easier to pull off."

I wanted to suggest that he just find somebody he already liked, but that ship had sailed. Auntie Bo had made up her mind. We were doing this.

For the first time in years, Maddox Mayhew turned to me and spoke an entire sentence. "I actually have to head over to the community center for my youth camp. I've got a photographer coming out today. So, maybe we could plan to get together after I wrap that up."

"You should take Mecca with you." Auntie Bo suggested. "Show her what you're doing over there with the boys. Give her an opportunity to see you, Busy. Get to know you."

Auntie Bo was not slick. I could see straight through her, with her "take Mecca with you" faced-ass. "I uhm, need to get back to work." I said.

Maddox nodded in agreement to my plan of going back to work. Part of me wanted to slap his gorgeous ass. He was so rude.

"You don't have to stay long." Auntie Bo, the meddler, assured me. "And I'll call Janaye and let her know that I sent you out on a little errand."

"Yeah, okay." He stood up from the sofa. "Well, I'm about to head out there now."

I stood up as well, choosing to ignore the smirk that was playing on Auntie's Bo's lips because she knew that she was getting her way.

Maddox and I were going to do this.

Here's the thing. Maddox and I weren't friends growing up, but I was very friendly with his grandmother, Miss Vera. Miss Vera didn't have any little girls in her immediate family. She and her husband had two sons, and when her sons procreated, they had given her three grandsons. On the other hand, Auntie Bo had eleven grand nieces, so feminine energy was at an all time high right across the street.

Miss Vera took advantage of that and was always spoiling my cousins, my sister and me. She was a gifted seamstress, and my cousins and I were her favorite fit models. She made us tons of little pink and purple ruffled Easter and "picture day" dresses. She was always having us over for impromptu tea parties, mani/pedi movie nights and stuff like that. She was a second aunt to us, so we all spent time with her in her home growing up. And while my cousins drifted away, as children do when they get old enough to discover life outside of the grown-ups they know, I continued to visit with Miss Vera, and spend time with her.

Before she got sick, and particularly afterward, I would go to her house on Sundays after church and watch Maddox's games with her. She never seemed sick when she was cheering for that boy. She would yell with such strength and vigor that I was sure he could feel her energy wherever he was in the country. She'd have me help her get decked out in her favorite jersey - a green one bearing his number, 27 and his name. She would bundle herself under her blankets and turn the television up way too loudly. When the Leopards won, it was a one woman ticker-tape parade and celebration. And if they lost? Miss Vera would spend half of the day looking like her man broke up with her to get with her best friend.

She was so proud of that boy. Proud that he'd set a goal for himself and reached it. Proud that he was talented, but even more so that he was hardworking and diligent. Proud that he avoided scandals and had a reputation as a nice guy with a good heart and a generous spirit. I knew "Busy" Mayhew through his grandmother's eyes, but I didn't know a damn thing about him otherwise.

I rode with him to the community center. I would've driven myself, but I didn't know where the "community center" was. We lived in Chicago...on the South Side, there was a community center on every other block. We ended up at The Dorothy G. Jackson Community Center, not too far from where we grew up. We were silent on the ride, neither of us said one word. Of course that was par for the course when it came to Maddox, but me? I'd always been a talker, so I didn't know why the cat had my tongue.

When we got to the building, I followed him through the facility and out to the back where they had a mini version of a football field set-up. The kids looked to be running plays, while a coach stood on the sidelines and called out instructions. The coach spotted Maddox right away, blew into his whistle and directed the kids to "take a quick five."

"Coach Mayhew." The guy said approaching us, his long legs making quick work of the distance.

Maddox slapped his hand. "What's up, Coach Ron?"

"Everything's good. The kids have been crushing those plays you showed them earlier this week."

"Good." Maddox nodded his handsome head. "Did the photographer make it?"

"Yeah, he's setting up. I was waiting for you to get here. He said that there's some paperwork that he needs you to complete."

"Paperwork?" Maddox's handsome face clouded over with confusion.

"Yeah." Coach Ron was clearly unsure.

"Where's he at?" As an after-thought, he turned to me. "I'll be right back."

Coach Ron and Maddox left me standing there while they went to find the problematic photographer. I walked down the sidelines and joined the young athletes at their bench.

"Who are you?" One little boy asked me. He had skin the color of graham crackers, big brown eyes, chiseled cheekbones, a very fresh low fade (like his mama knew it was picture day in advance) and a cocky demeanor. I could tell right away that he was going to be a problem for some lovestruck little girl in the future.

"I'm just visiting." I told him.

"Okay, because we don't have any girls on this team."

I looked around, realizing that he was right. "Well, why not?"

He shrugged his slim shoulders. "I don't know. But my last team had girls, and my pops pulled me off that team. Said I couldn't get the training I needed, if they had to dumb it down to include girls."

So, I knew right away that I didn't like his pops.

"There's nothing wrong with girls." I told him.

"And definitely not with you." A different little guy said to me, coming around the bench to get in my face. "I'm Jaylen." He smiled, showing me the cleft in his smooth chocolate brown chin.

I wanted to shake my head, because this had to be a team filled with future problem-starters for the female persuasion of their age group.

"I'm Coach Mecca."

"Coach Mecca?" The first little boy questioned. "I thought you said you were just visiting."

"I am. But that doesn't make me less of a coach."

"And you coach football?" Jaylen asked, still grinning at me, like he had confidence that he was going to actually pull me.

"I do not coach football." I admitted. "But I do coach athletes."

"What kind of athletes?" Another little guy asked.

"Talented ones."

"Can your athletes catch a pass?" Jaylen asked.

I shrugged my shoulders. "Depends on whose throwing it."

"Can *you* catch a pass?"

"You the quarterback?"

He nodded proudly.

"Show me what you got."

About eight of them followed Jaylen and me out onto the turf. They stood in a very formal formation, I just stood...somewhere. I listened to Jaylen say some random things

31

that obviously meant something to the rest of the offense, but meant nothing at all to me, then yell "Huuut."

I took off running. Jaylen had a good arm, he floated the pass, a surprisingly tight spiral, into the air and right to me. I caught it effortlessly (thanks to growing up with a twin brother who never seemed to realize that we weren't the same gender). Quickly, the energy on the field changed, and nine little bodies were heading for me, including the quarterback.

I was never the fastest runner, but as a highly trained dancer body control and movement were my specialties. I was able to out maneuver the kids and make it to the endzone without breaking a sweat. I spiked the ball, then did a little Milly rock, followed by some footwork, and finished my celebration dance with a little renegade.

I was smiling and feeling pretty good, when a voice boomed out over the bullhorn.

"Break time's over. Get in formation."

The children jumped, and sprang into action running off the field. I turned to see Maddox holding the bullhorn, looking stern. When our eyes met, he winked at me and grinned with his tongue sticking out. It happened so quickly that for a second I thought I'd imagined it, but when I looked back over at him, he winked, again. I walked back over to the sidelines, thinking *"uhm, so he has a silly side."*

Maddox

3

Luckily for me, Sydnie set everything up with the photographer. She even sent an assistant to make sure that we knew what shots to get, and everything. That was a relief, because I had no idea what images played best with an audience when you were trying to do damage control, after having your reputation murdered and outlined in yellow tape. Besides that, seeing Mecca on the field interacting with my athletes disrupted my focus. I knew she worked with kids, knew she was a dance teacher, but there was something about seeing her with my kids. It made me feel a way. I liked it.

I watched her standing on the field from the corner of my eye while the photographer's assistant went over the plan for the day. Mecca was undeniably pretty. Always had been, with her honey colored skin, and eyes that seemed dyed to match. Her cheekbones were high and sprinkled with dark freckles. She usually wore her sandy brown hair straight, hanging loosely at her shoulders, but today it was pulled up into a ponytail that gave her a youthfulness.

When we were kids, she was long and lanky, sprouting up the way most girls did during puberty, but tapering off just as quickly. She wasn't tall, now. She was 5'6 at most, and she wasn't skinny anymore, either. She had a dancer's body, but better. Mecca was slim-thick as hell. Sexy as hell. Fuckable as hell. I immediately tabled that thought. That wasn't what I needed to be thinking about. She was here to help me redeem myself, as a favor, not for me to try to bag.

I didn't know a lot about her, but I knew some, because she was my grandmother's favorite Watson girl. She was the one who would be at my house, hanging out with my grandmother in the kitchen when I came home from those grueling summertime practices in high school. She was also the one who would be at my grandmother's house when I would call after a game when I made it to the league. She spent a lot of time with my grandmother, in return my grandmother spent a lot of time talking to me about her.

"You know Pudding is graduating from Hampton University with a dual degree, dance and entrepreneurship."

"Pudding decided to go back to school. She's getting her MBA this time, Busy. Accepted to Northwestern. Smart and gorgeous. Plus she's choreographing for the NBA, now. She's doing big things, Busy."

"Pudding's graduating tomorrow, Busy. Remember I told you she was getting her MBA? She did it. Her daddy is throwing her a huge party out at his mansion. He's gonna send a car and driver to pick Miss Bo and me up and take us out there. I'm so proud of that girl. You should look her up on the social media, and congratulate her."

"Pudding's single now. You should send her some tickets to one of your games, Busy. You two could have a little reunion."

My grandmother was "un-subtle" as hell. I got the picture. She wanted to push me and *"Pudding"* together. I couldn't take that thought seriously, though. If she wanted me to get together with one of the Watson girls, she shouldn't have spent so much time pushing me away from them when we were growing up. I wasn't interested, so I never took any of her suggestions. Yet, it was like she was still trying to push me and Pudding into the same orbit from beyond the damn grave. And here I was, playing into it. Letting Miss Bo talk me into pretending like Mecca was my girl, bringing her to practice with me, fantasizing about having those strong dancer legs wrapped around my…What?

Cut that shit out. I told my subconscious. That was a problem I didn't need. Still, flirting with pretty girls had always been a character flaw of mine. I guess that's why when I caught the expression on Mecca's face after I yelled at my players, I couldn't help shooting her a wink, or laughing with my tongue sticking out.

"How old are your athletes?" She asked me on the ride back to my grandmother's house. I was surprised when her voice cut through the heavy silence of my truck. She hadn't said one word to me the entire time we'd been together, so I guess I was expecting that to continue.

"Eleven through thirteen."

"That explains it."

"Explains what?"

"Why a couple of them were so flirtatious."

I had to laugh. "They were flirting with you?"

"Not all of them. Actually, mainly just your quarterback."

"Jaylen Talib. He's...a lot."

"He has a good arm."

"He does." I agreed with a slow nod. "With the right coaching and work ethic, he could make some noise. So, your response to him flirting with you was to get him out on the field? A little redirection?"

"Basically, and some distraction while you and Coach Ron were dealing with the photographer."

"Is that what you do with your dance students?"

"All the time."

We were both quiet, but after a few seconds, she spoke again. "So, as far as this whole pretending to be your girlfriend thing, I'm not sure how you want to do this, and you probably aren't either."

I appreciated her saying that. It was insightful, because she was spot on. I had no idea how to do what I was supposed to be doing. I just knew that I needed to do it, and I needed to get it right. I was thankful that she understood that we would be making it up as we went along. I relaxed a little. And I mean, seriously, just a little. The whole situation still had me fucked up.

"Maybe you want to talk to your rep about it, what's her name?"

"Sydnie Whitmore."

"Did Sydnie tell you how and when we're supposed to start?"

"We can't start soon enough for Sydnie. She just really wants me to start with being as public as possible with you, as soon as possible, as often as possible. So, maybe dinner next week at Bistro MKC?"

"Uhm huhm. Okay" She agreed.

"And I've gotta text Sydnie your info and stuff tonight. They have to - vet you." I sighed. "Yo Mecca, this is so fucking awkward."

She chuckled. "Yeah, it is."

"I mean, we grew up together, but…"

"But not really."

"Right. So, I don't want to be all in your personal business, but if you think something is gonna come up in this background check that Sydnie's gonna run, I will not hold you to this. I don't want you to get embarrassed or feel exposed. I don't want you to get burned in any way from trying to help me out."

"I don't have an unsavory past, Busy. I feel pretty confident that I'll come back clean. You know I work with children, so I mean, I've supposedly been run through the FBI's database. I don't know what database your people are putting my name through, but I think it'll be fine."

We were both quiet, but I could feel her gaze bore into the side of my face. We were at a red light, so I made eye contact and gave her my undivided attention. "What's up?"

"Should we address the elephant in the room now, or should we wait until later?" She asked me.

"What's the elephant in the room?"

"The fact that we grew up together, but not really. We've known each other forever, but I don't know you, Busy."

"It's weird that you would say that, and then call me 'Busy', because the only people who ever call me that, are people who've known me since I was a kid."

"Well, your grandmother called you that, and I knew her. I was close to her."

I nodded in agreement. The person behind me started to honk their horn. Chicagoans - they were impatient as hell on the roadways. I pressed the gas pedal.

"What was the deal with you treating us the way you did growing up?"

"How do you feel like I treated you and your cousins growing up?"

She sucked her teeth, and even though I couldn't see it, because I was watching the road, I knew she rolled her eyes. I could feel it. "You don't know what I'm talking about?"

"I do." I admitted. "I know that we weren't friends…"

"You completely ignored us."

"So, we're doing this." I muttered mostly to myself, but with her proximity to me, there was no way she didn't hear what I said.

"Don't you think it's time? I mean, especially if we're gonna pull off this whole ruse. Because right now, I don't even know if I like you." She paused. "That's a lie, right now, I feel like I don't like you."

"Damn, I thought Clarke was the one that didn't pull punches."

"Family trait."

"Okay, let's do this. When we moved in with my grandmother full-time, I was ten years old. Yeah, we knew each other before then, but just in passing. We would see each other if we happened to visit my grandmother at the same time you all were visiting your aunt."

"I'm not talking about when we were babies. I'm talking about when we were old enough for it to matter. I wouldn't hold something that you did when you were six against you, Busy. But see, if you knew me...you would know that."

"You're big mad about this, huh?" I asked, realizing for the first time how much my behavior had affected the girl from across the street.

She didn't respond. Truthfully, I didn't really need her to, I could tell where she stood.

"By the time I moved in with my grandmother, I had discovered girls. And you and your cousins...let's just say that I had a lot of impure thoughts about y'all. One day, my grandmother caught me trying to get...fresh, for lack of a better term, with Kyndall, and she pulled me to the side. She told me in no uncertain terms that if I wanted to 'dilly-dally' with some young girl's emotions, to leave the Watson family out of it."

"Uhm."

"As I got older, if she caught me looking at one of you all - and full disclosure Mecca, I did look, and think about, and dream about you all. Anyway, if she caught me looking, she would give me the same speech. After awhile, I got tired of hearing the speech, so I put you, with your pretty face, Indigo with them big breasts, Joya with that fat ass, Kyndall with that beautiful smile, and Clarke with her kissable ass lips into a little box that said "do not touch" and I stayed away from y'all. Clearly you took it as a personal offense, but it wasn't. It was self-survival. I was running through women, and I knew my grandmother would've killed me, if I had treated a Watson girl the way I was treating other girls."

"I don't get what that has to do with you ignoring us for all of these years. We're grown now, Maddox. I have seen you numerous times. Numerous. And so have my cousins. You still barely say three words to us."

She had a point.

"I think it's just become a habit, honestly. A bad habit, Mecca. A rude habit. And I apologize."

"You owe everybody an apology."

39

"You're right." I agreed, because she was right. "I'm an asshole. Believe me, that has been made clear to me, as of late."

Neither of us spoke for a bit.

"Anyway, Joya is having an anniversary party."

"How long has she been married?" Joya was one of her first cousins.

"I think this is their 5th anniversary."

"When is it?"

"Saturday. If you want to come, I'll bring you. We can take some pictures together, post them on social media. We can have Indigo post them on her Instagram."

"Indigo's like famous now, right?" Indigo was another first cousin, who was currently making noise on social media.

"She's a popular beauty guru on social media."

"She's dating Northern McKinley, the music producer, too? I see them on my Instagram feeds all the time."

"She is."

"Cool. I'll go to Joya's thing with you on Saturday, and on Friday, there's something I need you to do for me."

"What's that, Busy?"

"Friday there's this charity event that I need to attend, it's part of my image overhaul. Sydnie wants me to take you as my date. It's an industry thing, so she wants me out there, front and center. Sorry, it's last minute."

"This whole thing is last minute. I'm not tripping. It's formal, huh?"

"Total black tie. Again, sorry."

"Don't apologize. I love dressing up."

That shocked me, and I don't know why.

"I hope you love *paying* for formal gowns, expensive designer shoes, hair appointments...and nail appointments." She teased.

"Uh, not necessarily, but it is what it is. I got you. Just tell me what you need."

"I need for you to finance my fly, so I can help you look like you got Ainsley Neuberg outta your system. Duh."

Mecca

Maddox's team moved fast. Thursday morning, by the time I had showered, dressed, done my skin care regimen and pulled my hair up into a neat ponytail, I had a text message from Maddox's younger brother and attorney, Brandon. He let me know that the non-disclosure agreement and contract that I needed to sign were in my email inbox. I texted him back.

Me: **What's up, Brandon? I'll have my attorney look over the documents. If he thinks they're good, I'll sign them and get them right back to you.**

The thing about Brandon Mayhew, was that I considered him a friend. Although Maddox had made it his business to ignore the Watson women while we were growing up, the same couldn't be said for Brandon, or their youngest brother, Xavier. I didn't know if Miss Vera relaxed her rules after Maddox, or if Brandon and Xavier were just rebellious enough to ignore them. Whatever, they were cool with all of the Watson girls. At one point, Xavier was in a serious relationship with one of my younger cousins.

Brandon: *Mecca baby, I can't believe you're even doing this for Busy's ass.*

Me: *Me either, but Auntie Bo…*

Brandon: *Yeah, he told me. Lucky ass*.

Me: *Stop flirting.*

Brandon: *Nope. You're too pretty not to flirt with.*

Me: *If that's the case, why'd you spend all your time sniffing up behind Indigo when we were kids? You were enamored with the light-skin.*

Brandon: *What? You're light skinned.*

Me: *I'm caramel colored, Sweetheart. Indigo is high yellow. That's what you like.*

I teased him, because it was true.

Brandon: *Doesn't matter now. She's hemmed up with dude. So, let me shoot my shot with you.*

Me: *Leave me alone, Brandon.*

I knew he wasn't serious. That was how we related to each other, with teasing and fake flirting.

Brandon: *So, who all are you telling about the arrangement with Busy? I would hate to have to sue your pretty ass...but I will.*

I laughed out loud at that.

Me: *Immediate family only. I have to tell my parents, and you know I can't keep nothing from British. She already knows.*

Brandon: *You gonna be able to keep it from the rest of the pretty committee?*

The pretty committee was how Brandon and Xavier Mayhew liked to refer to the Watson girls.

Me: *Yeah. His secret is safe with me, but you might want to draw up an NDA for British. You know she has a mouth on her.*

Brandon: *You're right. I'm about to text her right now.*

I took British with me when I went shopping for a formal gown. We went to an obscure

little boutique in the Gold Coast area called, Saturated, that my mom liked to frequent when

she had an event that she needed to *dress* for. The owner, Georgette Luckett was a

ground-breaking, barrier busting black model in the 1970s. She knew fashion and had an

eye for all things beautiful. When she retired, her daughter, Greer had taken the helm, and

she was just as impressive as her mother. When I told Greer that I was going to a benefit

with Maddox Mayhew, NFL free-safety, she pulled about twelve gowns for me.

"So," British said, pawing through the gowns on the rack that Greer set aside for me. "I

get that Auntie Bo asked you to do this, and I know how you are about old people."

I chuckled. British teased me constantly about all of the time I spent hanging out with

Miss Vera and Auntie Bo.

"But what else besides that made you agree to do this?"

"Nothing." I said, fingering the luxurious material of a dreamy silver gown.

"Just Auntie Bo? It had nothing to do with the fact that Busy is fine as hell, or that those

football pants can't hide his dick print?"

"I'm pretty sure that's an athletic cup in his football pants, Brit, so there's that."

She tilted her head to the side. "Maybe, but I've been looking at Busy's dick print since I was a senior in high school - it ain't always been an athletic cup. Plus, he loves to thirst-trap in those compression shorts on his IG page. Just saying."

I shook my head, not just to ward off what she was saying, but to clear the thought of his dick print from my mind.

"It wasn't the dick print?" She confirmed.

"No, British. It wasn't the dick print. I don't even pay attention to his dick print." I pulled a black gown from the rack and held it out.

"Lies. You've always had a crush on him. Since we were little, you've had a crush on him."

I started separating the dresses that I wanted to try on from the ones that I knew weren't going to work for me.

"I did have a crush on him when we were little. Then it faded." I looked over at my younger sister, and it was obvious from her facial expression that she didn't believe me. "I'm not lying, Brit. I wouldn't lie to you. If I was digging him, I would tell you. I'm not. He was my teenage crush, and I haven't been a teenager in a minute."

"So, no feelings for him at all?"

I cut my eyes at her and smiled slyly. "Now, let's not be ridiculous. Have you seen him? Of course there's feelings." I ticked them off on my fingers. "Feelings of lust. Feelings of hunger. Feelings of…"

"Horniness." She supplied.

"There are those."

"You think you're going to be able to convince people that you guys are a real couple?"

"Girl, people believe anything they see on the internet. All he needs is some strategically placed, suggestive pictures of us together, and the media's gonna be like, 'Who's the mystery woman on Maddox Mayhew's arm?'."

"Just make sure that he's not out there in "suggestive" pictures with other chicks. You don't wanna look like a member of his line-up."

"Yeah, I had my attorney put that in the contract."

"I'm excited to see how this plays out." She told me.

That surprised me. "Really?" I raised my eyebrows. "Why?"

"I don't know. I feel like he was always destined to end up with one of us Watson girls. Why shouldn't it be you?"

"I can't imagine that I'm Busy's type. I would imagine him with somebody more like Clarke or Joya."

"Clarke?" Her brown eyes were wide in surprise. "Uhn uh. Not at all. He's motivated, focused and high energy, like daddy. You're motivated, focused and high energy, like mama."

"And on that note, I'm gonna try on these dresses." I took three dresses from the rack and headed towards the back of the boutique. I wanted to keep things professional with Busy. I didn't need British planting any seeds in my head that I wasn't trying to nurture.

Maddox

4

I paid for Mecca's benefit attire, but she took her sister with her when she went shopping, so I had no idea what to expect. When I picked her up Friday night, I was nowhere near prepared for what I saw. My heart raced wildly in my chest, its rhythmic thumps resounding in my ears when she answered the door for me.

"I'm almost ready." She told me, and turned on her heel to walk away, but then she stopped, and gracefully turned back to me. "You must see something you like, but you need to close your mouth before you catch a fly, Busy. I know Miss Vera raised you better than that."

I closed my mouth.

She'd selected a white dress. It was clingy, and lacy, and sheer, and form fitting, and it made two very distinct thoughts pop into my head. The first was that I wanted to touch it, and the second was that I wanted to touch it while taking it off of her.

"She did raise me better than that, but Miss Vera never saw you looking like this, Pudding." I called after her.

I heard her chuckle from wherever she was in the condo.

"So, what's this benefit?" Mecca asked as I opened the door of the truck for her and helped her out of the backseat.

"CTE. It's for a foundation that was created by Jennifer Zuriela. Her husband, Jack, was the quarterback for the Pythons for almost ten years. When he left the league, things got...crazy for him."

She nodded. "I've heard about the consequences of CTE; mood swings, aggression, depression." Shaking her head, she pulled in air through her teeth. "Scary."

It was my turn to nod. "Yeah, he committed suicide, left his money for research on the condition and Jennifer started the foundation."

"Are there gonna be a lot of NFL people in here?"

"Yeah. That's why Sydnie really wanted me to come. Get my face out there, in front of the people who matter, in a positive way."

"You know I've been going to these kinds of events with my parents since I was little. Just in case you're worried about me, don't be."

I looked down at her like she was crazy. "Trust me, I'm not. Ain't nobody in here gonna be paying attention to your behavior, they're gonna be too busy looking at your body in this dress that I'm pissed off you tricked me into buying."

"I didn't trick you." She objected, her pretty brown eyes big with dismay. "I texted you a picture of it from the boutique."

"I saw it on the hanger, Mecca. It looked like a bed sheet or some curtains or something. I didn't see it on your body. If I'd seen it on your body, I would've said 'hell nah, pick something else'."

"You don't want me to look good?"

"Not this good." I shook my head. "Not in front of this crowd."

She giggled, and it was a tinkly sound in the warm night air. "For fifteen years, you ignore me. Now, you wanna be on some protective big brother stuff."

"Ain't nobody trying to be your big brother in that dress, Ma." I said honestly.

"Well, if those are the vibes this dress is giving off, then I say it was money well spent." She looped her arm through mine.

"The vibes that dress is giving off are giving me a hard dick." I muttered to myself.

Mecca and I walked into the ballroom with her holding onto my arm. The place was done up to impress the moneyed crowd that Jennifer invited. There was a lot of silvery, shiny, and sparkly shit everywhere you looked. I wasn't paying attention to my surroundings, though. I couldn't stop glancing down at her cleavage. Mecca's body in that dress was perfection.

While I was busy looking down at her cleavage, somebody said her name.

"Mecca B. Goode, check you out - pimping the hell outta that dress."

I snatched my eyes away from Mecca's breasts and looked into the face of Curtis Starrveld. Curtis was a defensive back for the Falcons. I couldn't say that I disliked him, he was just *that* dude. The dude that was always a little too loud, always too over the top, always needed to draw attention to himself.

Mecca gave him a smile that seemed genuine. "Hey Curtis."

He grabbed her free arm, pulling her body to his. Her arm slipped out from mine, leaving the obvious absence of the warmth of her body.

I tried not to let myself get tight when his hands drifted down and didn't stop until they were right above the line of scrimmage. That was when I noticed that the damn dress was backless.

Yo, I fucking hated this dress!

After the hug went on longer than I was comfortable with, which honestly, would've been two seconds, I spoke. "Yo Starrveld, I'mma need you to stop being so damn handsy with my girl." His back was to me, and Mecca's face was somewhere by his chest so neither of them saw how my face involuntarily frowned up at me calling her my girl. I didn't know where the terminology "my girl" had come from, but I could admit that seeing him all over her made me feel possessive.

"Sorry, my dude. Me and Mecca go way back." He said as a way to explain his blatant violation.

49

And before I even thought to edit myself, I responded, "I don't give a damn if y'all go back to the fucking womb, don't be holding her like that." I put my arm around her waist and pulled her to me, my face still arranged into a mean frown.

She looked up at me, her eyes were warm and calm. She wasn't taken aback by my behavior. "You ready?" She asked easily.

I nodded stiffly.

She turned to Starrveld. "Take care, Curtis. See you around."

"Yeah, can't miss you in that dress, Shawtie."

This motherfucker. I thought to myself as I watched him walk away. Once he was out of my line of sight, I released Mecca, and walked away myself. She followed me.

We ended up outside, on one of the patios overlooking one of the gardens.

"Busy." She said my name patiently, like she caught my hand in the cookie jar, after repeatedly telling me to keep it out of there, but was still amused.

"Yo, I'm sorry." I said not turning around to face her. "I ain't mean to embarrass you in front of your friend. It was just him, and you, and that fucking dress..."

"You did what you were supposed to do. If I was really your girl, there's no way you woulda let him hug me like that. If we want this thing to work, you have to treat me like I'm really your girl. Besides, everybody knows Curtis' ass is a creep. I don't ever want him touching me."

I didn't respond, I was too far in my own head, wishing that I could rewind time. I would've slid right in front of dude's ass, and not let him lay a finger on Mecca.

She leaned close to me. "Can we have a quick 'getting to know you' session?"

I finally turned around and faced her. "Yeah, let's do that, Pudding."

She smiled at my use of her nickname. "This dress," she gestured to the dress that I hated, but that looked so good on her. "Is not my usual style. It's very...flimsy, and thin, and sheer. This dress is for you."

"For me?" I asked, screwing up my face. "Well, we can burn that motherfucker the minute we get back to your place. I fucking hate that dress. It's a shit starter, and I already know I'mma have to whup somebody's ass behind it."

"This dress is to show the people that you need to show that I'm an upgrade for you from Ainsley Neuberg. When your girl looks good...you look good."

I shook my head at her words. "You coulda came up in here wearing a tank top, leggings and Jordans and you woulda been an upgrade." I paused. "Because you're an upgrade. And thanks for caring about making me look good."

She nodded. "Oh, what I was saying before about this dress."

I looked at the offending, yet alluring garment.

"This dress is thin. Like, really thin. It's almost like having on lingerie in public. I would prefer it if nobody else hugs me tonight." She looked up at me, with those honey colored eyes. "You up to being in charge of that? You're good with man to man coverage, right? Think you can cover my body from all of these thirsty dudes?"

"I can definitely cover your body." I said out loud. In my mind I said, "I'll do any fucking thing you want me to do to your body...in or out of that dress."

Later that night, it became clear that I really didn't understand what I'd signed up for when I told Mecca that I would cover her body. She knew a lot of people at the benefit. Correction, she knew a lot of players at the benefit. I didn't trip, because I understood that she'd spent two years choreographing for an NBA team, and the last five years choreographing for both the NBA and the NFL. She knew players. That didn't bother me. What bothered me was the way that basically every dude who approached her to speak,

51

looked at her in that dress. And they all wanted to hug her. I was blocking motherfuckers left and right. Got called a hater a few times, too, but I didn't care. Mecca said that she didn't want no thirsty dudes pressing up on her, so none pressed up on her. Except for me. I pressed up on her every opportunity that I got, I mean, all in the vein of making it believable that she was my new love interest.

When we got back to Mecca's building that night, I left Heavy in the truck, while I walked her up to her unit. I stood behind her, taking in the dips and curves of her bare back and the cut of the dress, as it barely skimmed the top of her ass.

She unlocked the door, pushed it open and turned around to face me. The way she was standing, halfway inside her darkened condo, her right hip popped forward, that white dress draping so naughtily over her body, made me lick my lips.

Damn! I thought to myself. If she was actually my girl, she would have been halfway out of that dress already. When I noticed that her eyes were trained on my mouth, I involuntarily licked my lips again.

"Thanks for tonight, Busy." She said, managing to drag her eyes up to meet mine. She motioned for me to come inside her place. "Thanks for making sure all the creeps, freaks, and opportunists didn't get the chance to feel me up."

I chuckled. I had felt her up enough for everybody during the course of the night. My arms had been draped around her shoulders while she stood in front of me, as we talked to a local radio DJ that we both knew. I kept her pulled close to my side as we browsed the items that were available through the silent auction. I rested my shoulder against hers, as we sat at the table and ate dinner with my colleagues.

Each time some dude approached, trying to love her up by way of greeting, I pulled her into my body, usually full frontal, shook my head and said, "Not today, Dawg. No hugs today. You just need to wave." Each time I pulled her close, she seemed to melt into me - fold her body into mine until we were flush. Whatever vibe we were giving off, it seemed to work. Eventually, dudes stopped trying to hug up on her.

"Thanks for letting *me* feel you up all night."

She cut her eyes at me. "Right? You were a little handsy. Halfway through the evening, I was thinking that your grandmother must be dancing in Heaven. She stayed trying to scheme on ways to get us together like we were tonight."

I laughed out loud at that. "Are you serious? She was giving you that smoke, too? I swear, everytime I talked to that lady she was making up some excuse for me to contact you. I can't believe she was doing the same thing to you."

"That's because you haven't seen my collection of Maddox "MayDay" Mayhew jerseys. I got a new one every Christmas and on my birthday." She plopped down on the couch, and started fiddling with the buckle on the five inch heels she wore.

I sat down next to her, scooped her ankle into my hands and worked on getting the shoes off of her.

"How many #27 jerseys do you have?" Her shoe was off, and I was rubbing her foot, because there was no way those shoes didn't have her in pain.

"Uhm, maybe twelve."

I stopped rubbing. "Get the fuck outta here." I said in disbelief.

"Apparently, I'm your number one fan." She chuckled, with a shrug of her shoulders.

"After tonight, I'm definitely *your* number one fan. Thanks for looking out, Mecca. You don't have to do what you're doing." I took a beat and grabbed her other foot. "Or do it so well."

"Have you checked your notifications? I'm sure after the way we were boo'd up tonight, somebody has posted something somewhere."

"Yeah, true." I sighed. "You gonna be okay?"

"You got me, right?"

"No doubt. If the bullets start blowing, I'll take that heat."

She narrowed her eyes at me. "I'm gonna need you to keep that same energy tomorrow."

"At Joya's anniversary thing?" I asked, not understanding.

"Yeah, uh huh, at Joya's anniversary thing."

Mecca

5

So, I lied to Maddox. I didn't care about the energy he took to Joya's party. I cared about the energy he took to my parents' house, because that was where we were going. I had Maddox arrive at my condo at 3:00 on Saturday, knowing full well that we weren't expected at Joya's until around 5:00.

"Hey." He said, when I opened the door for him.

My heart did kind of a pitter-patter. He was such a gorgeous man. The night before, when he showed up at my house wearing that tuxedo that accentuated every ripple and arc of his muscular frame, I wanted to skip that benefit and have my way with him right here, in my own bedroom.

He looked like a man in that tux. I mean, I knew Busy as a scrawny, ashy little boy, and also as a handsome, moderately mature teenager. Even when I watched him play professional football, all I saw was an oversized kid, having fun and doing what he had always loved to do. But last night in that tux, I saw Maddox - the grown ass man. The way he held me, pulled my body close to his and protected me from being groped and manhandled had me seeing him in a whole new light.

"Damn." He said, walking past my kitchen into my combination, living room/dining room where he was confronted with a beautiful view of Lake Michigan and Navy Pier. "Million dollar view, huh? I didn't see this last night, your blinds were closed."

"Yeah, it is a beautiful view." I agreed. It was the view that had me lusting after a unit in this particular building off Lake Shore Drive for almost a year, fantasizing about what it would be like to actually call it home.

On my 25th birthday, my parents surprised me by gifting me the down payment, and money to furnish the place. While I knew in my heart that you weren't supposed to love material things, I couldn't help loving my place, at least a little bit. It was so...me.

"Can we sit down and talk for a few minutes?" I asked, making my way over to my stone gray sofa and hoping he would follow.

He did, dwarfing my sofa. I looked over at his big hercules ass. When did he get so damn delectable? The smooth, chocolate brown skin that reminded me of brownies fresh out of the oven. Intense dark brown eyes, the kinky fade, the manicured beard, the kissably full lips, the gigantic biceps that were straining against the fabric of the moisture-wicking henley, and the dimples. Why did he need the dimples, when he was already panty-melting without them? That was just overkill. Delicious, beautiful, unfair overkill.

I wasn't a frequent flyer when it came to dating. That was more my little sister, British's style, but I went on dates. Dudes came over and sat on my sofa from time to time. I mean, even my twin brother, Cairo, and my daddy who were both over six feet tall sat on it, but Maddox's big, muscular ass had my sofa looking like it belonged in Barbie's Dream House or in her beach bungalow, like toy furniture or something.

After too long, I realized that while I was thinking impure thoughts about him, he was waiting for me to talk.

"Uh, so, Brandon emailed me the contract."

"Yeah, I heard. Sydnie finished her background check, too."

"Did I come back clean?" I teased.

"You came back exactly the way I would expect a goody-two-shoes to come back."

"Goody-two-shoes? Is that what you think of me?"

"More so before I saw you in that dress last night." His head was down, reading and responding to text messages.

"That dress really made an impression on you, huh?"

"How many times do I have to tell you that I hated that fucking dress?"

"Sure didn't look like that to me." I couldn't help commenting.

"Yo, that dress looked good as hell on you...and that was my main problem with it."

"And I thought your main problem last night was keeping your hands to yourself."

His head flew up, and our eyes locked. He cocked his head to the side. "Are you trying to get something started, Mecca? I mean, you're sitting right next to me on this baby ass couch, clearly you don't realize how little effort it would take for me to pull you into my lap if you want this work. You wanna see how much of a problem I was having keeping my hands to myself last night?"

I blinked rapidly, surprised that he took things there and by how his words put butterflies in my stomach and made my vagina grow warm. Of course I wanted that work, all those muscles pressed up against me? Hell yeah. Legs in the air, mouth wide open humming his name? Yes, please. But I wasn't here for that. Couldn't be here for that. Busy and I were doing business. We needed to keep things on the level.

I licked my lips. "You can keep that work to yourself...for now, Busy."

He grinned at me, showing me the dimples that I found so attractive. "For now?"

The tension that had amassed in just those few seconds between him asking me if I wanted "this work" and me responding, seemed to dissipate.

I grinned back at him. "I said what I said."

He watched me for a few seconds, his eyes sweeping over my face and landing on my eyes. Then he searched them, like he was trying to decipher some secret code that was lost inside my irises.

I broke the eye contact first. "I went on Instagram today. Saw the pictures from the benefit."

"Oh yeah?" He turned his attention back to his phone.

"Yeah, I kinda had to after Clarke called me this morning cursing me out about them. She had a lot of questions."

"I got four words for you: Don't. Read. The. Comments."

"Yeah, Clarke read some of them to me. The ones she read weren't too bad. I'm sure she skipped the ones where I was getting dragged."

"Fuck those people." He said dismissively waving his imaginary haters away with his hand. "They don't know you, or me and if I see some shit like that, I'm airing motherfuckers all the way out. How are you feeling about Joya's thing? You feeling like we can pull this off in front of your cousins?"

"Yeah, we just need to make sure that we stay leveled up." I sighed heavily.

"What's up? Why're you sighing like that?"

"We need to talk to my parents, Busy. I can't mislead them. I can't have them thinking that I'm in some serious relationship with you, when it's just an arrangement. A ruse. And knowing my mother, the social media junkie, she's been on Instagram today, and has already seen the pictures." I paused. "Here's the thing, my father enjoys being difficult with the guys we bring home. I'm not just talking about me and British, either. I mean, all of my cousins, all of the Watson girls and the girls on his side of the family. He doesn't like the guys any of us introduce him to, and he won't like you.

Don't waste your time trying to win him over. Don't compliment me, or try to be charming or anything like that. He shuts that kind of thing down, rudely. Just be polite and treat me with respect in his presence. You need to appeal to my mother. Compliment her, but not too much, that will only piss off my dad. Oh, and we need to pick up flowers. You need to bring my mother flowers."

"That's a lot of damn rules, Pudding. When do we need to see them? Will they be at Joya's thing?"

"Nah, that's just for the cousins. We have to ride out to my parents' house...in Winnetka."

"And where does Joya stay?"

"Lincoln Park."

"From downtown, to the suburbs, back to the city."

I winked at him. "Hope you gassed up."

"Oh, and I'm driving?"

"Yes, sir."

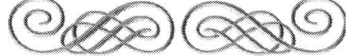

In the vein of being the hostess with the mostest, when Janaye Goode found out that Maddox and I were headed to their house, she put out a spread. She had a taco bar set up on the island of her chef's kitchen.

"Mom, you did too much." I told her, as I took in the bowls filled with pulled chicken, strips of steak, ground turkey, diced onions, chopped tomatoes, guacamole, sour cream, pico de gallo, shredded cheese and sliced limes.

"It's fine, Mecca. Fix plates and come into the dining room so we can talk. Your father's been nervous all day, worrying the heck outta me about what you could want to talk about.

I didn't tell him that I saw you in my Instagram feeds, looking all...cozy with Busy Mayhew. Now, here he is...standing in my house with you. I'm intrigued, daughter. Hurry up, fix plates." She prompted and flitted away from me.

That was another thing my mother did, she flitted.

After Maddox and I fixed ourselves plates on my mother's good China, we met my parents in the dining room. She had already placed the flowers Maddox presented her with at the front door, in the middle of the table. That was good. But my father was wearing a frown on his handsome face, that was bad.

"So, everybody knows each other." I started off stating the obvious. "You both know Maddox - Busy, lived across the street from Auntie Bo, before he left for college. And Busy you know my parents."

"It's nice to see you both, again." He said politely.

So far, so good.

"Okay," I blew out a deep breath. "The other day, Auntie Bo asked me if I could come over to her house. When I got there, she asked me to do Busy a favor, because he's had some...challenges in the public eye, lately, and..."

"Challenges?" My dad guffawed. "That's what we're calling them?"

"That's what they are, Bryan." My mom said, giving Maddox a warm look and reaching over to pat his arm. "He's young. He just lost his grandmother. He's made some missteps." She shrugged her shapely shoulders. "It happens."

"Okay." My dad acquiesced with a short nod of his head, then turned his eyes on me. "What do *his* missteps have to do with you?"

"I'm getting to that, Daddy."

"Get there faster, MeMe."

I nodded at him, ready to take the plunge and just spill the whole story, but Maddox held up his hand.

"These are your parents, but this is my situation. I can level up." He winked at me. "I'll take it from here."

"Oh, you'll take it, huh, big guy?" My father's eyebrows were practically touching his hairline. "Okay, the floor is yours."

"I was mourning my grandmother's passing while simultaneously denying that she had passed, and I found myself behaving in ways that were outside of my character." Maddox began. "I'm not proud of the things I did...the mistakes I made. Actually, I'm embarrassed by them. But yo, it's out there on the internet, and most of the videos went viral, so, yeah. Anyway, as a man, all I can do is press forward. My management rep suggested a few things that would help put the spotlight back on my positive moves, instead of focusing on my fu...mess ups. Finding a nice young lady, and giving the appearance that I'm settling down is one of the suggestions. Miss Bo asked Mecca if she would do me the favor of acting as my partner/lady friend, while I put my reputation back together, and Mecca was gracious enough to agree to help me."

I had to admit that Maddox was much more succinct in telling the story than I would've been.

My mother looked at me with wet eyes. "MeMe, I'm so proud of you. You're such a sweetheart."

"I don't know about all that, mama." I said honestly. "I'm saying, I wasn't immediately here for helping Busy. You know he's funny acting. Auntie Bo kinda had to twist my arm to get me to agree to help him."

My father laughed out loud at that. Then he spent several seconds that felt like hours, quietly moving his piercing gaze between Maddox and me. "Busy, I've always liked you."

I practically choked on my soft-shelled taco. Since when did Bryan Goode like any guy that he wasn't related to by blood?

My father continued. "I've admired your self-discipline since you were a kid. My daughter thinks you're 'funny acting', but I know better. I know it wasn't easy ignoring my daughters and nieces - day after day, year after year. There are a lot of them, and they're all beautiful. I was a teenage dude once, I know the types of thoughts that run through the minds of pubescent boys. But you didn't shit where you ate, and that was impressive. I told your grandmother once, that with that kind of self-control, there was no way you weren't gonna make it to the pros.

I can't say that I'm surprised that if Bo was doing the picking, she would pick MeMe to play the part. Bo and your grandmother have been shoving you down Meme's throat for at least the last six, seven years."

Trust my father to always keep it a buck. No discretion whatsoever.

"I understand why they thought they could match-make y'all, though. You and MeMe are a lot alike. The focus. The drive. The self-control. She's a dancer, self-discipline is her life. You're an athlete, same exact story. Either one of you let your self-discipline slip...your career's in jeopardy. You know that first hand, Busy, you're living it right now.

The thing you gotta know about Mecca is that she's loyal, and genuine. She'll stand by your side, ten toes down. But her patience for fuckboy antics is low. She's the type that will back up your bullshit in a crowd, but when you get to the car...she'll fuck you up about that same bullshit. I encourage you to stay on her good side and leave any fuckboy behavior at the door.

As her father, I can't help but notice that this whole deal seems incredibly one-sided. I mean, you get a trophy 'girlfriend'," My dad shot me a wink. "And the opportunity to repair the damage to your rep, what is Mecca getting out of this?"

"I'm just doing it as a favor to Auntie Bo."

"Treat my daughter with respect, man. While she's playing this role, do your part. Leave the other chicks alone. No pictures, no videos, I don't even want whispers of you with other chicks. Like zero, man. I don't want my daughter embarrassed or made to look like a fool. I don't want your 'challenged' reputation traded for hers. I don't want her dragged on social media while you sit back quietly looking out for yourself. This is a favor, it should be treated with the appreciation that comes from knowing that she didn't have to do this for you. She could've let you figure something else out, or blow in the damn wind."

"I've already told Mecca, if the bullets start blowing, I'll take that heat."

"Well, I guess if bullets start blowing, we'll see, won't we?"

Maddox nodded his head.

"Busy, as I've said before, I've always liked you, but that shit is totally inconsequential if you bring bullshit to Mecca's doorstep. Please. Please. Don't make me fuck you up over my daughter."

Maddox was quiet when we left my parents' house. I wasn't sure if it was because my father was so...himself or what. Still, when we pulled up in front of Joya's place, I turned my body to face him.

"So, pulling this thing off in front of my cousins."

His eyes met mine. "You seem more worried than you were at your spot. You got any suggestions?"

"I don't know. I would say just be yourself, but since 'yourself' would typically ignore me...can't do that." I joked.

He smirked. "I think the stage of me being able to ignore you has passed. Think I'll be myself."

"Good luck with that."

As I moved to get out of his truck, he grabbed me by my wrist. I turned around and gave him my attention.

"So, when I'm being myself, are you gonna roll with it?"

Busy was a double-whammy - that deadly combination of being flirty and understanding exactly how sexy and desirable he was. My mind (or maybe it was my vagina) started thinking all kinds of thoughts with that question. "I don't know. You're not gonna be backing me up against any walls, and kissing me in the mouth are you?"

His eyes raked over me, and he licked his kissable lips. Those juicy, kissable ass lips. "Maybe. Is that what you like? Being backed up against walls, Mecca?"

The way he looked at me, the way his big, strong hand held my wrist with restrained power, the way his pink tongue traveled over his brown lips so slowly, made me fluttery in the stomach.

"I like a lot of things." I told him.

"I'mma need you to keep that same energy when I'm pressed up against you in front of your cousins."

Inwardly, I was a tiny bit shook, because if I wasn't mistaken, he had just promised that there would be moments where his big, sexy, muscular body would be pressed up against mine. Can't lie, I definitely hoped that there would be 'backing me up against walls' involved. Outwardly, I did my best to appear unbothered, though. "And you just make sure that if you're backing me up against walls, that you're ready for what comes next." I pulled my wrist from his grasp and turned away from him humming Lizzo's "Truth Hurts."

Nasir Payne, Joya's husband answered the door for us holding the couple's youngest daughter, two-year-old Lyric.

He grinned when he saw me, his handsome face lighting up. "What's good, Mecca?" He pulled me into a one-armed hug, releasing me slowly when he noticed Maddox standing behind and off to the side of me. "Mayday Mayhew?" He asked in surprise, calling Maddox by yet another nickname.

Maddox stepped up, with his hand outstretched. "Ay, what's up? Nasir Payne, right?"

Nasir nodded, his face still scrunched up in shock. He took Maddox's hand, and gave him the universal "black man" handshake. "Yeah. Come on in. Come on in."

Nasir and Joya were young and wealthy and their lifestyle reflected that. They lived in one of the most expensive and coveted neighborhoods in Chicago. Lincoln Park was about a mile from downtown, and right on the lakefront. It was within walking distance of parks, shopping, restaurants, the zoo, the botanical gardens and museums. Their house was on a quiet, tree-lined, family friendly block and was simply gorgeous. It was a semi-open floor plan with exposed brick walls, and historical details. Classic, but modern.

We stepped into the foyer, and Nasir led us through the living room, the dining room, past the kitchen and the large family room out to the spacious deck on the back of the house. There were people everywhere, but I spotted my family members right away. Joya, sitting in the flyest one-person porch swing I had ever seen, cradling her four year old daughter, Honor in her lap. Clarke, Cairo and Nasir's youngest sister, Torri were at the bar. My cousin Indigo and her guy, Northern McKinley were on the loveseat. British, and two of my other cousins were chilling on the sofa.

I walked over to Joya with Maddox on my heels. "Oh my goodness, big baller. Where the hell did you get this swing chair, porch-swing-for-one, whatever you call it? It's so nice."

Her light brown eyes went really wide as she moved the antsy toddler out of her lap. "Pretty sure I got it from Wayfair. Where did you get your...guest? Hey Busy Mayhew. Long time no see."

"What's good, Joya? Congratulations. Five years."

"Thank you. What brings you to my humble abode?"

"I was invited, and since I spent so many years showing the Watson girls unnecessary and undeserved shade, and I knew you would all be here, it felt like the perfect opportunity to offer one, big collective apology."

Immediately the deck got quiet as hell. In the words of my Aunt Bo, you could've heard a mouse pissing on cotton.

"So, let's hear it." Prompted Clarke. "And it better be good. I mean, we've waited long enough for it."

"Right." Indigo agreed.

"I apologize for the way I acted when we were growing up. You all were always cordial and friendly, and instead of returning that energy, I was…"

"Rude as fuck?" Clarke supplied.

"Aloof?" Joya tossed out.

"Obnoxious?" British chimed.

"Arrogant as hell?" My cousin River asked.

"Distant?" Kyndall questioned.

"Well, fuck." Nasir said loudly. "What the hell was going on over on 72nd and Paxton back in the day? Next door neighbors was sworn enemies and shit?"

"Basically." I mumbled.

"I won't say we were enemies, but Maddox Mayhew definitely wasn't checking for my cousins." Joya told her husband.

"No, he wasn't." Clarke agreed, giving him the evil-eye. "He barely spoke to us. Any time he was forced by his grandmother to be in the same room with us, he spent all of his damn time looking over our heads. I don't know what the hell was on the ceiling, but it was obviously more interesting than us. I'm surprised he can recognize us or tell us apart from each other. He never *looked* at us."

That was when Northern McKinley stood up and walked over to Maddox. He extended his hand, with a smirk on his handsome face.

"What's up, dude? I'm Northern, nice to meet you." Northern leaned in close and said something that was only meant for Maddox's ears.

Maddox laughed out loud, nodded, then shook Northern's hand. "Good to meet you, too, Northern." Then he gave his attention back to the Watson women. "You're right, Clarke. You're right. And I apologize. I was young, and dumb. And as Mecca has since pointed out to me, there were so many other ways I could've handled that. I chose the wrong one. I fucked up. Please forgive me."

I took that as my cue, moved closer to Maddox and put my hand inside of his, giving it a squeeze.

"Uhm, looks like somebody already forgave you." British commented.

"Thankfully." He pulled me into his side, hugging my body to his. I looked up at him, not even trying to do it "adoringly" or whatever the hell Sydnie Whitmore suggested, but when he looked down at me and our eyes met, something moved in me. Like, I felt like maybe he meant it when he said he was thankful that I forgave him.

"Nah, Mecca just finally figured out what it was all along." Cairo said from where he was chilling at the bar. "That Busy couldn't afford to pay attention to y'all, because you're distractions."

"Gorgeous, distractions." Northern added.

"Distractions who would've fucked up his head, when he needed to keep his head in the game." A dude that I didn't even recognize said.

"Dudes. They don't even know him, and they're jumping in to take up for him, about why he showed us so much shade back in the early 2000s." Clarke sucked her teeth.

"But we're men, Clarke. So, when he's trying to talk around it, so you won't start to feel a way, we understand what he's not saying." Nasir explained.

"I understand what he's not saying, Nasir. He couldn't get caught up in romancing one or two or all of us, because first of all, Miss Vera would've put her foot up his ass. Secondly, how was he supposed to choose? I mean, we're all fucking show-stopping."

That comment received catcalls, and shouts of agreement from every corner of the deck, including from me.

"And third of all; that would've made things mad awkward if there was a bad break-up or a teenage pregnancy or something, since we were neighbors. We get it. We could've gotten it when we were in high school. The thing is, instead of just keeping it a buck, he…"

"Ugghhhh." I said, holding up my free hand, the one that wasn't encased in Maddox's massive paw. "Can we let it go? What's done is done. It's the past. Busy messed up." I cut my eyes at him. 'I think he gets it. You're not about to keep riding his ass about it, Clarke."

She eyed me. "Why? Is it your turn to ride his ass, Mecca?"

Again, catcalls and shouts came from every corner of the room. But this is what we did. This was what it looked like when the Watson girls got together.

"Not this very second." I said, once the chatter had died down. "But maybe when we leave here. Meanwhile, get off my man."

"Your man?" That was my cousin, Reign.

"I said what I said." I assured her, as British caught my eye and gave me an almost imperceptible nod. I looked up at Maddox, who was surprisingly, looking down at me. "Let's get food."

He followed me into the kitchen. There were people in there, so we couldn't talk, and I really wanted to talk to him. I quickly fixed him a plate containing everything he pointed at, then threw about two things on a plate to call my own. I led him to a semi-hidden alcove under the stairs, that the Payne family clearly used as a mud-room area. I sat down on the built-in bench, that doubled as a place for the family to store shoes and boots and such.

"How do you feel?"

He looked over at me in confusion. "What do you mean?"

"I mean, with Clarke coming for you."

"Pssshhhtttt." He was dismissive. "You do know that I'm familiar with Clarke, right? Actually, I'm kinda more concerned with them coming for you."

"For me? My cousins? Nah, that's not gonna happen. Yeah, they're gonna tease me about you, then act like they're jealous that after all of these years, I was the one to *finally* pull you, but they're not gonna like, come for me for real or nothing." I paused. "They love me."

"I knew you would drag Busy over here to hide from the crowd." British said dipping into the alcove to join us.

I shrugged my shoulders as I took a tiny bite of potato salad.

"You okay?" She asked gently. "Clarke's ass."

"No, I expected that." I admitted. "Especially from Clarke."

"What about you, Busy? You get what you expected?" She smirked.

"Actually, I got less than I expected. I expected to be roasted all night."

"With Mecca standing there?" She rolled her eyes. "No way that was happening. If you wanna pull this thing off, especially in front of my family, you need to learn your girl."

"You the tough guy in the family, *Pudding*?"

I looked over at him. Apparently, teasing me tickled him, because he was grinning and showing me the dimples that caused panties to moisten from coast to coast.

"I thought that was Clarke." He continued, before I could answer the original question.

69

"Clarke is the toughest talker, but when it comes to fisticuffs, it's Joya and Reign that bring that heat." British cut her eyes at me. "And *Pudding*. Trust me, your girl is nice with her hands. Plus, she got that mama bear thing happening. You know, from always having to take up for me, Clarke, Indigo, River and Reign growing up."

"You a street brawler?" He asked, biting into his brisket sandwich. I didn't get how he could possibly still be hungry after slamming like, at least 10 tacos at my parents' house, but he was eating again.

"I'm a boxer. Took it up to help build strength. Dancers tend to have extremely strong legs, I wanted to have...good arms."

"Sexy arms." British corrected. "Tell the truth, and shame the devil. After she saw some old school movie with Angela Bassett playing some chick named Tina something..."

"Tina Turner?" Maddox couldn't stop laughing. "How old are you, British?"

"Leave me alone, Busy."

"She's 25. That's why her age is showing." I said.

"Anyway, your girl wanted sexy arms like that." She continued.

"Let me see." Maddox told me.

I flexed my bicep, then turned my arm and straightened it, so that he could see my tricep.

He whistled appreciatively, then reached out and gingerly ran his hand along the skin of my arm. I tried not to shiver.

"Damn, looks good, Mecca. You got definition like a motherfucker."

"So, are y'all still *pretending* to be involved? Cuz Busy is looking like he wants to pounce on you, MeMe."

I sighed heavily at her comment. What I didn't want or need was British watching us and judging our behavior. We needed space to figure out how to "be" with each other. I

70

stood up from where I was sitting. "We should go back to the deck before somebody else comes looking for us."

Maddox stood up, and the three of us started for the deck.

"What took you so long to get here?" British asked, as the three of us rejoined the rest of the guests.

"We went out to Winnetka." I told her.

I said it in my usual tone, but you would've thought I yelled it with the way that all of the other conversations on the deck seemed to die on people's lips.

"What?" I asked the group.

"You took Busy out to Winnetka?" Indigo looked horrified, she knew exactly what was in Winnetka. "Why?"

I couldn't really tell them why, and I couldn't pretend like it was to introduce Maddox to my parents, since they'd known him forever.

I shrugged my shoulders. "We were out running errands." I lied. "So, we went out there and had lunch with them."

"I wanna know what DJ B. Goode had to say about you and Busy. What? Dating?" Joya said.

"He said that he's always liked Busy."

"He likes Busy? Uncle B. doesn't like anybody." Indigo reminded us.

"Apparently, except for Busy." Kyndall commented. "What did he say, exactly? Just, 'I really like you, Busy'?"

"He said that he's always admired Busy's self-discipline." I told them, leaving off the tidbit about Busy not shitting where he ate.

Maddox

<u>6</u>

A few hours later, after spades, bid whist, and dominoes had died down, Mecca was standing in a circle of her cousins talking. I walked up behind her, wrapped my arms around her waist and bent over to whisper in her ear.

"Don't tense up." I told her, although from my body language anybody watching us probably thought I said something intimate. "Keep that same energy you had in my truck."

"Uh uhm." She breathed out on a tiny chuckle, playing her part.

"Even when I do this." I said, then slowly bobbed my head down to her neck and breathed her in before I let my lips gently brush against her skin. Her skin was so soft. And she smelled like...something I couldn't quite put my finger on, but it was delicious. Edible.

"I'll keep the same energy." She said quietly enough, so that only I could hear. Then she shifted her body, and pressed into me. If she wasn't wearing those sexy ass, high heeled sandals, there was no way that she would've been tall enough to subtly rub her ass against my dick the way she was doing. "Just don't try to seduce me, Busy."

I pulled her tighter. "Not trying to seduce, just trying to make sure we're believable."

She turned around to face me, my arms still around her waist. I looked into her pretty face, into those bright, brown eyes. She smiled at me. I could've stopped myself. I mean, I was known for my self-discipline, but I didn't stop myself. Didn't want to. So, I dipped my head down and kissed her neck again.

She let out a soft exhalation, almost like a tiny sigh and wrapped her arms around my neck. I liked the way she sounded and felt, so I kissed her neck again.

"Get. A. Room." British chided.

Those within hearing distance chuckled at us.

Mecca slowly pulled away, still looking up at me, her eyes glassy. "We should get ready to go."

73

I shot a quick glance at my watch. It was after midnight. "Yeah." I agreed. Then, I whispered in her ear. "You know your cousins are gonna think that we're leaving to…"

"Get it in? Yeah, that's the idea." She confirmed. "Uhm, we're leaving." She announced loudly. "Nasir, can you let us out?"

The first thing Mecca did when we made it to her condo, was to toe her way out of those sandals she was wearing and exchange them for fuzzy slippers. The second thing she did was to prance into the kitchen.

"I need water. You want water?" She called out to me.

"Sounds good." I replied, lowering myself onto her couch. Her couch was nice, but for some reason it seemed undersized. I had a hard time getting comfortable on it.

She walked in the room carrying two bottles of water, and handed me one. Setting her drink on the cocktail table, she sat down with me.

"Busy, I know we talked a little about our arrangement before…"

"Don't trip, Mecca. We're gonna have to talk about it again, and again. We're probably gonna have to redefine and recreate it again and again. This situation is weird as hell. I don't know what to expect. You don't know what to expect..." I trailed off with a shrug of my shoulders.

"I have...concerns."

74

That made me look up from where I had been checking notifications on my phone. Indigo had posted pictures of Joya's event on her IG, and there were already comments about how "cozy" I looked with Mecca. The look in her eyes made my heart thump unexpectedly. I placed my phone on her cocktail table. "What's up, Mecca?"

"I know you don't know me, but I know me."

"Okay."

"Today, when you were pressed all up on me…"

"Did I make you uncomfortable? I was fucking with you, but I didn't mean to make you uncomfortable."

"I'm not uncomfortable with you, Busy. I know that my cousins and I give you the business about not knowing you and you being a virtual stranger and all of that, but I know the important stuff. I'm confident that you're not some creep. Miss Vera raised you to be a gentleman. It's not that. It's more that, when you touch me like that…you're a man and I'm a woman. My mouth and my brain can say that this is an arrangement, but I'm worried about my body responding to yours."

Was it wrong that it made me happy as hell that she was having concerns about her body responding to mine? Because earlier, when she pressed her ass into my dick, all I could think about was how fucking good she felt.

"Is this too much for you?"

She smiled at me. "The look on your face, Busy. Stop frowning like that."

"Yo, you're doing me a favor that you don't have to do. If it's too much, if you feel uncomfortable, then I'll ask somebody else."

"You know there are already pictures of us floating around on IG. I don't think it would help your reputation to be boo'd up with me today, and boo'd up with someone else next week."

I didn't give a shit about those pictures. I needed her to be cool. I needed to not put her in a bad situation. "Fuck that, Mecca. Sydnie will have to figure something else out."

"Calm down." She placed her hand flat against my chest. At the contact there was a little spark, a heat. "I'm not trying to back out on you, boy. I just want you to...look out. Like, if you notice my nipples getting hard or something, don't take it as a personal challenge. Don't tease me."

I couldn't stop the grin that spread across my face, if I wanted to. Not that I wanted to. "Oh Pudding, there is no way in hell that I'm agreeing to that. If I *ever* notice your nipples are hard, because of something *I'm* doing to you, I'mma have to celebrate that shit."

She rolled her eyes as hard as she could. "This is why we were never friends as kids."

"But we're about to be very good friends, as adults."

"We're about to act like it, anyway."

"Nah." I shook my head. "We're about to become friends. We're gonna be spending a lot of time together."

"I'm gonna have to get used to you touching me." She said, cutting her eyes slyly at me. Kind of making me feel like she didn't think that was the worst thing on earth.

"Touching you, pressing up against you, rubbing you...backing you up on walls or other hard surfaces." Shit. I was turning myself on.

She rolled her eyes, again.

"Yo." I got serious for a second. "Honestly, you've gotta know that it's not one-sided. I'm saying, my grandmother raised me to be a gentleman, but Ma, I am a man. I got sensations in my lower regions. When you were rubbing your ass against me earlier today, I was kinda worried about you getting poked."

Her face was the picture of innocence; eyes wide, mouth pulled down in a sad, yet sexy pout. "What?" She asked.

"Whatever, Man." I told her.

"I'm not a man."

My eyes raked over her body, which was covered by a deep yellow t-shirt that she had knotted at the waist, and minuscule denim shorts. She was preaching to the choir.

"Nah, Mecca, you're definitely not a man."

"Stop looking at me like that, Busy." She said in a scolding tone, but the glint in her eyes told me that she was teasing.

"Looking at you like what?"

"Like you wanna be more than friends."

"Stop trying to get something started, Li'l mama." I stood up from her sofa. "I'mma get outta here. Before I go, I'm thinking church tomorrow morning, dinner Monday night, and the banquet for my youth camp on Friday night. You wit' it?"

"Yeah. I'm pretty sure I'm with it."

"And we'll talk about the weekend later."

"What's this weekend?"

"Every year, somebody on the team throws a big barbecue before we head into training camp. This year the backfield is hosting."

"In Kentucky? We're going to Kentucky?"

"If you can swing it. I mean, I know you have your own commitments. Classes to teach, a business to run." Sighing, I continued. "You've been nothing but accommodating, Mecca. I'm not trying to take advantage of that, or take your help for granted. I mean, weekends seem like they're probably prime time for dance lessons."

"They typically are." She agreed with a nod. "But summers are slower. Dance usually runs with the school year, so we don't offer many classes during the summer." She winked at me. "That's when DJ B. Goode and Janaye like to vacation."

Chuckling, I nodded.

"But, it's also when I'm in the highest demand for choreography. So, I'll have to look at my schedule to make sure that I'm not out of town, but off the top of my head, I think you're good."

"A'ight, I'm out."

Mecca followed me to the door, when we arrived I pulled her into my arms for what was supposed to be a quick, friendly hug. Instead, I found myself looking down into her pretty face; her eyes soft, her expression open, her lips pink and lush. And I had the inexplicable desire to brush my mouth against hers, to capture her lips and see if she tasted as sweet as I imagined she did.

She dropped her head into my chest, breaking the eye contact, effectively breaking the spell she had cast on me.

I released her from the embrace. "I'll see you tomorrow."

"Tomorrow." She repeated, unlocking and opening her front door for me.

Mecca

When my mom strutted into my office on Monday morning, I wasn't even surprised. I knew how Janaye Goode operated. She'd probably spent the entire weekend worrying my father to death about the "Busy/Mecca" situation. Smirking to myself, I watched her lithely fold herself into the chair opposite my desk.

"Good morning, daughter."

"Hey mom." I replied, unable to wipe the smirk from my face.

"So, tell me about ..."

Before she could complete her thought, British burst into my office. As graceful as my mom was, British was equally as inelegant, making her way through life doing her best impression of a bull in a china shop.

"What are we talking about?" She asked, closing my door with a resounding click.

"What are you doing here?" I asked, giving my younger sister the screw-face. "It's 8:30 on a Monday morning, shouldn't you be at your own place of business?"

With her hands up in a sign of surrender, she assured me that was her plan. "I'm going, I'm going. I stopped by to talk to mommy...now I want to talk to you. Did you ask her about Busy?" She addressed that question to our mother.

"I was just about to. So, what's happening with you and Mr. Mayhew, Mecca? Is the *arrangement* working out?"

Raising an eyebrow, I questioned, "why'd you say *arrangement* like that? Like we're doing something inappropriate."

"Not inappropriate, just...undercover." She clarified.

"And have y'all been under the covers?"

My eyes involuntarily rolled to the ceiling at British's comment. She had absolutely no chill. "Ugh."

My mom chuckled, though. I didn't know if it was because British was her baby or what, but she always thought British's outrageousness was cute.

"All jokes aside," my mom continued. "What's going on with the two of you? For you to have been on the outs for all of these years, you seem awfully friendly."

"Nothing's going on with us. I'm basically just trying to get to know him. And yeah, we've never been friends, but I've known him forever. I can be cordial with him."

"It's more than cordial, MeMe." British assured me. "Ma, you should've seen them at Joya's house. They were all over each other."

"We were not!"

With a hard side eye, and her arms folded across her ample chest, she begged to differ. "You kinda were."

I flashed-back to Busy kissing me on the neck, and my subsequent ass-rubbing-against-the-pelvis response. She was right, we kinda were all over each other. "We did that to convince the rest of the family that we're really together."

"Worked like a charm. With all that bumping and grinding, I know you had to smoke a cigarette in the car."

"Ahhh." My mother laughed out loud. "Seriously MeMe, how are you supposed to resist all of that lusciousness? I mean, you're only human and Busy is a big old piece of chocolate."

"Fine, sexy chocolate. Muscular chocolate. Goatee, kissable lips, big di…"

"British!" I censured.

Her face was the picture of decency. "What? I was gonna say big dimples." Her brown eyes narrowed slightly. "What did you think I was gonna say?"

My mother was tickled pink by our interaction. "Yeah MeMe, what did you think she was gonna say?"

"Ugh!" I let my head fall into my hands. Family could be so aggravating.

"Seriously baby," my mother's eyes gleamed with love and hopefulness, "you and Busy are a *very* good look. And your dad was right when he said that you two have a lot in common."

"Who wouldn't be a good look with Busy, though? He's gorgeous." I allowed.

Nodding in agreement, British spoke. "That he is. So, spill the tea, girl. Are there any sparks flying?"

I sighed heavily. How to answer that question? Be honest? Coquettish? Aloof? Disinterested? I couldn't be dishonest with my mother and my sister, so I put it out there as plainly as I could. "I'm attracted to him. He's so handsome, it's impossible not to be. And that body."

"Yaaasssss, sis. It's that body. All of those muscles, covered by that smooth chocolate." British's eyes were glazed over, like her body was present, but her mind was far, far away.

"What about his heart?" Trust my mother to cut to the chase.

"He was raised by Miss Vera, no doubt he has a good heart." British insisted. "I mean, he paid for MeMe's attire when she went to the benefit with him. No questions asked, and didn't even blink at the $3000 she spent."

My mother was quiet, but her gaze held mine hostage. She always had the power to look into my eyes and see into my soul. She could read my heart and my mind without me having to say a word.

British was oblivious to the silent conversation that was taking place right in front of her, she just kept chatting away. "Speaking of the benefit, how did that go?"

"It was good."

"What did Busy think of the dress?"

"What *did* Busy think of the dress?" My mother seconded. "Because from what I could see on Instagram, that was quite a dress."

"That dress was a mess." I admitted.

Apparently, British and that dress were homegirls or something, because she was personally offended. "That dress was everything - dreamy, lacy, ethereal, form-fitting…"

"Sheer. I don't know why I let you talk me into it."

"Because you looked like the hotness in it."

"Because I was practically naked!" I insisted.

My mother easily brought the conversation back around to where she wanted it. "Did Busy think you were practically naked?"

I chuckled at her lack of subtlety. "All night long he kept repeating how much he hated the dress."

British couldn't keep herself from reacting. "He hated the dress?!?"

"Said it was starting mess, and that he thought he was gonna end up having to fight somebody over me...in the dress."

A slow smile crept across my sister's pretty face. "Uhm, you have his nose wide open already?"

"It wasn't like that." I maintained.

"What was it like?" My mother with the questions.

"I think he's just been...conditioned to look out for us, the Watson girls, and take care of us. I think Miss Vera kind of insisted on it."

My mother studied her fingernails like a word from Jesus was coming through on her nail polish or something. She picked at an imaginary hang-nail as she spoke. "Did he have to take care of you at the benefit?"

"Well, there were a lot of athletes at the benefit, and you know how presumptuous and cocky they can be - thinking that everybody wants them. And I had on that dress. I didn't want any random, thirsty as...dudes rubbing all up on me or touching me under the guise of getting a hug. So, I asked him if he would make like a football player and "cover" my body."

"Make like a football player and "cover" your body?" British repeated. "Well dang, my sister's a boss. Was he like, 'hecks yeah, I'll cover your moth..dang on body'." She caught herself.

I laughed at her silliness. "Pretty much."

"He spent his night fighting guys off of you?" My mother asked.

"He wasn't fighting them, mom. He was just...encouraging them to move around."

British's eyes were as large as saucers. "How?"

"He told them that I wasn't giving hugs, and if they wanted to say hello, they could just wave."

Clearly, Busy's comedic stylings were on par with Kevin Hart, because at that, British was on the floor with laughter.

"He told them niggas to wave. Sorry mama. I just can't believe he told them to wave."

British's glee was apparently contagious, because soon, both my mother and I joined in her laughter.

Friday night after the youth camp banquet, Maddox and I hopped into the back of his Range Rover. After spending three days with him in one week, all I could say was that each time had been more fun than the time before it. And the banquet was a blast.

Maddox and his team had outdone themselves. They'd rented out a local venue, and transformed the place, having it decorated to resemble the ESPY awards complete with a few of his NFL friends acting as presenters and announcing the "winners" in each category. There were film clips of highlight moments, "golden" statuettes, a press room, a red carpet and it was catered with the most delicious food I ever tasted. I looked at him with a new appreciation for the man he was, and how he got down.

"That banquet was so nice, Busy." I told him, as we made our way downtown towards a late dinner with the professional athletes who had come to the banquet. "It's obvious how invested you are in your athletes and your program."

He placed his hand on my thigh, giving it a firm squeeze, and demanding my attention, his eyes met mine. "Thanks for coming with me, Mecca. Thanks for making me look good."

His eyes held a double entendre. Sydnie Whitmore had made sure to get the local press out in force to cover the banquet as a "hometown hero/feel good" story. The coverage was good for the boys who attended the camp, but it was also good for the players, and especially for Maddox. Playing the role of his doting girlfriend made him look good. The strapless, yellow Carolina Herrera mini dress and five inch Tori Burch sandals that I was wearing made him look good. I got it.

"You're welcome."

A comfortable silence settled over the truck, Maddox thinking his own thoughts, and me wondering if he had always been this person - this selfless, sweetheart of a guy - even when I disliked him and thought he was an arrogant asshole.

We seemed to be the last ones to arrive at the restaurant. Heavy pulled up just in time for us to see Maddox's younger brother, NFL wide receiver, Xavier Mayhew and three other guys disappear into the door of the eatery. Heavy jumped out of the truck, and quickly opened Maddox's door, allowing him to slide out.

I waited as Maddox walked around the truck, swung open my door and extended his hand to me. "You ready?"

"Yep."

Xavier was the first person to greet me when we walked into the private room for dinner. He pulled me into a breath-snatching embrace. I returned the love, even though a small part of me had beef with him for the way he played my little cousin, Reign Champion, back when they were dating. Still, he was like another little cousin to me, having watched him grow up from the time he was 3 years old, until he went off to college.

"I'm kinda tempted to cuff ya ass right now, just to make your boy go off." He whispered into my ear.

"Don't do it." I cautioned him with a chuckle. "You'll traumatize me. I can't imagine getting felt up by little Xavier Mayhew."

"I'm not so little anymore. Ask about me."

He released me from his grasp, and I took a quick second to give him the "up-down." He wasn't lying. Little Xavier Mayhew was all grown up. "I don't need to ask about you, you're standing right here in front of me."

"And I'm grown." He stated, like he still wanted me to give him my stamp of approval.

"You're grown, and very handsome."

Grabbing my hand, Xavier walked us over to the table and held my seat while I sat down.

"Back off, Little Dude." Maddox ribbed him good-naturedly.

Xavier took the elder Mayhew's razzing in stride. "You mad because I'm pulling out her chair? You better level up, before I leave this restaurant with her."

Maddox was dismissive in the way that only older siblings could be. "Whatever, man." He sat down next to me and made the introductions, pointing to each man as he named him.

85

"Yo Mecca, this is Kolby Foz; Justus Alexander, Robeson Miller, that's Lance Gardner and you know X's ass. Ay, this is my girl, Mecca Goode."

"I don't remember you being how we're doing it in the Chi?" Robeson Miller flirted. "Hell, I might need to come home more often."

I simply smiled.

"Don't get your ass ripped at this table." Maddox warned.

Robeson clearly wasn't one to stand down easily. He completely ignored Maddox's threat. "So, gorgeous, how'd you meet this burly, swoll motherfucker?"

"We grew up across the street from each other." Maddox supplied.

Robeson gave him the screw face. "Who asked you, Dox? I'm talking to her. I hear your scratchy, Barry White ass voice all of the time. I'm trying to hear something feminine. Let her talk."

"Next time bring your own girl."

"Next time, she might be mine."

That was when I spoke up, with a shake of my head. "No, I won't be yours. I'm too busy being his."

That must've been the right thing to say, because Busy leaned over to me and whispered in my ear. "Oooh shit, *Pudding*. Don't fuck around and make me forget we're pretending up in here."

Maddox

7

Heavy dropped us off at Mecca's place after dinner. I noticed that once again, the first thing Mecca did when she entered her condo was to start working on removing those sky-high sandals.

"You got, like an aversion to high heels, but you stay wearing them." I commented.

She looked at me and nodded like she didn't understand my point. "High heels make my legs look good. They accentuate the calf muscles, and emphasize the curvature. They just hurt like hell."

"Newsflash Pudding, you've got some sexy ass legs. You don't need to torture yourself with twelve inch heels. Your legs would look sexy in high top Converse."

She hit me with the million-dollar smile that I could definitely get used to, as she padded past me in her bare feet. "Thanks, Busy. Be right back."

I made myself comfortable on her sofa until she returned, wearing black biker shorts and a cropped Hampton University t-shirt.

Fuck! I thought to myself. Why did she have to be so sexy? And why couldn't my mind stop replaying what she'd told Miller at the restaurant.

"I'm too busy being his."

I shook my head slightly to clear it and patted the sofa next to me. "Come sit down, and I'll rub your feet. I know they hurt after those sandals."

She sighed heavily, as she made her way over to the sofa and plopped down next to me. "I'm a dancer, my feet always hurt. Doesn't matter if I'm wearing high heeled sandals or gym shoes."

I pulled her right leg into my lap, trying not to get distracted by the silky smoothness of her honey colored skin. I wrapped my hands around her foot.

"When you hang up your cleats, you should follow your true calling and become a certified masseuse." She practically moaned, which between her foot in my lap, how sexy she sounded and how relaxed she looked made me have to adjust myself, because my dick was trying to grow.

"Yo, there's something I always wanted to ask you ever since we were shorties on the block."

Her eyes were closed as she enjoyed the sensation of me rubbing her foot, but she slowly peeled them open. "What's that?" Her voice was raspy, choked with placidity.

"What the hell did you used to spend all that time talking to my grandmother about?" Mecca's body quivered with laughter.

"I'm not saying she was boring or anything," I continued, "but you would be over there for hours and hours. I thought that was the weirdest shit when I was in high school." I tapped her leg lightly, so she knew to put her right one down and give me her left one.

She placed her left leg in my lap. "Oh man, I was over there getting wisdom. Between your grandmother and Auntie Bo, I learned how to be a woman."

Well, that shit was intriguing. "What do you mean?"

"They just poured into me. I could talk to them about anything. Anything. And I did. I think I told your grandmother when I lost my virginity."

"Straight up? That's weird, Pudding. I didn't even tell her when I lost mine."

She chuckled. "Your grandmother and Auntie Bo would listen and give advice, but they weren't judgy. I've had a lot of messed up experiences in my life, and they walked me through all of that."

"Like what? Or is it too personal?"

"Like why I decided to take up boxing. Everybody thinks I took it up, because I wanted sexy arms like Angela Bassett in *What's Love Got to Do with It*, but I'm not that vain."

"But you let people think that?"

"To be honest Busy, one of the biggest lessons your grandmother and my great aunt taught me is to not give no fucks about what people think. They can think what they wanna think. I used to suffer from nice-girl syndrome, like a lot of women do. I wanted people to think I'm nice, to like me. Now, I'm on some, take me as I am or kiss my ass...quick."

"Why'd you take up boxing, Mecca?" It was more than curiosity. It was the perverse need for her to confide in me, to share things with me that she hadn't shared with many people.

"Basically because I got tired of being groped by fuckboys and creeps. When I told my parents that I was going to pursue dance as a career, the first thing they did was make me enroll in self-defense classes. That's because my mama had her fair share of scary experiences when she was a video dancer back in the 90s, and my father couldn't always be available to whup ass or do security. She took self-defense, so they made me take self-defense. The first time a dude groped me after I finished my self-defense classes...I froze up. I couldn't think of how to do any of the techniques. He took my lack of action to stop him as my permission."

"Damn."

"That is like, the number one thing they drill into you when you take self-defense classes. That the possibility of you freezing is very real. I never thought I would freeze, though. I had mentally played out what I would do in a situation like that, and it did not include freezing up. But when dude touched me, it was like I had an out of body experience. I could see his lips moving, knew he was talking slick to me, but I didn't hear the words. All I could hear was my brain shouting for me to do...something, but I was frozen."

"What happened?"

"I danced with the band, in these little skimpy, revealing ass costumes. Somebody was always getting touched, propositioned, or grabbed. I wasn't a frequent flyer, because I was the only black girl on the team, which made me invisible to most of the white boys on that campus.

There was this one dude, though. Running back on the football team. The motherfucker must've been feeling himself that day. He grabbed my ass and kissed my lips. But when he pulled me to him, and I could feel his penis pressing all on me, I snapped out of it. I still didn't go into self-defense, though. I mean, I went into defense of self, but I didn't go into self-defense techniques. I just went crazy." She chuckled humorlessly. "I went smooth South Side. Balled up my fist and went straight ham. He was shocked when he caught these hands. My punches were garbage, but he wasn't expecting them, so they were effective. As soon as the opportunity presented itself, I kneed him in the nuts, and ran.

Of course, I called my mom and told her what happened, and how I froze up. I was embarrassed, and disappointed in myself. I went into a shell after that incident, didn't like being anywhere on campus alone. My mom was like, '*you need more self-defense classes.*' My dad said, nah. He told me that if I was willing to box niggas to get away from them, then I should learn how to box niggas. He came to campus about a week after the incident, with about five of his goons, took me around town and found me a gym."

"Come through, DJ B. Goode. I would've done the same damn thing for my daughter. Except, I would've beat dude to a bloody pulp."

She eyed me curiously. "That's what the goons were for."

"Dudes left you alone on campus?"

"I ended up having to transfer out of Wheatin University. I mean, I accused one of the most celebrated football stars of violating me, then my black daddy showed up and showed his ass. He blessed out the administration. Had his lawyer draft letters to the school president, the board of trustees and the alumni association. Then he came on the yard and the next day campus security found dude's bloody, battered body in the parking lot of an apartment complex just off campus? Everybody knew what happened to dude. Who happened to dude. That campus became a very uncomfortable place for me to be. I couldn't get out of there fast enough. Your grandmother never told you that I was invited to leave Wheatin?"

"Nah, I mean, she told me that you graduated from Hampton University, but I thought that's where all of this took place."

"That happened at the PWI - the predominantly white institution. After that, I transferred to Hampton. I needed to be able to look around and see some faces that looked like mine."

"I'm assuming that things went better at Hampton."

"And you'd be wrong." She stated flatly. "Athletes, frat boys, fuckboys - different school, same crap. For whatever reason, some men think that they have a *right* or something, to touch women's bodies at their whim."

I wanted to be surprised by the information, but I couldn't be. I knew dudes, had spent the majority of my life in athletics. I knew how easy it was for some to develop a false sense of self and of worth. I knew how patriarchy could lead them to believe that anything they decided they wanted was supposed to be theirs. For a lot of dudes, women were so far down the list of things that were important, that they barely saw them as humans. I'd been in more conversations than I cared to remember where men talked about women like they were merely walking vaginas with beautiful faces, and mouths that talked a lot of shit.

"Things were better, but there were still times when I had to get belligerent. When I had to use boxing and self-defense techniques, the old...1, 2 punch."

"Haha. Corny ass." I told her.

She laughed at herself.

"You're so corny."

"I thought that was cute." She admitted.

"You're cute, but what you just said...nah." I tapped her leg lightly, so that she knew to remove her leg from my lap. My semi-hard dick was deflated like a motherfucker. Talking about perverted, rapey assholes had that effect on me. "So Kentucky. Tomorrow afternoon. Do you need me to pick you up?"

"Do you think that would be easiest?"

I looked over at her, staring unabashedly. Apparently the intensity of my gaze made her uncomfortable.

"What?"

"Nothing. I'm just wondering why I never knew you were this...congenial. Things with you are really, really easy."

"Is that not what you're used to?"

"Not at all." I stood up from the couch and stretched. "I'm used to a frustrating, crazy push-and-pull where everything is a struggle."

She eyed me suspiciously as she stood from her seated position. "Seems like you need to date a different caliber of women."

"Yeah, I do...and if anybody asks, I am." I winked at her. "I'll pick you up at 4:30."

She stretched, going up on her tip-toes, and giving me a look at the definition in her calves. I shook my head in appreciation.

"You've got some sexy legs, Mecca."

"Are you a leg guy?" There was a wicked gleam in her pretty brown eyes.

"I think I'm a "Mecca" guy."

She chuckled as she pushed me lightly on the forearm. "Stop playing, Busy."

I caught her by the wrist and pulled her lithe body to mine. "Ain't nobody playing."

She looked up at me, curiosity filling her expressive eyes as they bounced between my eyes and my mouth.

"We gotta dilemma."

"What's that?" She whispered breathily.

"I wanna kiss you right now, but…"

I didn't get to finish my thought, because Mecca reached up, wrapped her hands around the back of my head and pulled me down until our lips were touching. At first contact, I knew I needed more. I swept my tongue into her mouth, intertwining it with hers. While my tongue explored hers, my hands found her perfect ass and cupped it bringing her body even closer to mine. I deepened the kiss, plunging my tongue into her mouth, my grip on her ass so possessive that I lifted her off of her feet. She wrapped her sexy, powerful legs around my waist and kissed me passionately until the need for oxygen overtook the desire to connect with one another.

She rested her head on my shoulder, panting lightly. "Uhm, your grandmother is probably doing the Holy Ghost two-step right now."

"Probably." I chuckled, setting her down on her feet. I stared down at her. "How did I ever manage to avoid you?" I hadn't meant to say it out loud, but apparently, my mouth didn't get the memo.

"I don't know."

"Me either." *Stop staring at her like a fucking creep*. I chastised myself. "Uhm, so I'll call you around 4:30 when Heavy and I are downstairs."

"Okay."

I followed her to the front door, where she turned around to face me, placed her open hand against my chest and gave me a smile. "See you tomorrow, Busy."

I couldn't stop myself from bending down and placing a gentle kiss on her pouty lips. "Later, Pudding."

Mecca

94

By the time I got Busy's big, sexy ass out of my condo, I had so much repressed energy that I didn't know what to do with myself. I tried sitting down on the couch, but I couldn't shut my mind down. Finally, I broke down and pulled out my phone. There were a gang of women in my family. I mean, not only did I have my mama; her four sisters, and her two sisters-in-law; I also had ten first cousins who were female; and a younger sister. I could call any of them, and get advice, encouragement, love, wisdom or understanding. But there was really only one person whose counsel I wanted on the Maddox Mayhew situation, so I Facetimed her.

Her pretty face appeared on my screen. "Hey MeMe. What's up?" She whispered. It was after midnight. I knew it was probably too late to be calling her, but I needed to talk, and it was either her, or my mother. And I definitely didn't want to have to talk to Janaye Goode about wanting to get with Maddox Mayhew.

"Did I catch you at a bad time?"

"Who is that?" I heard her husband's sleepy voice ask.

"It's MeMe."

"What's up, Mecca?"

"Hey Nasir."

"Let me go in the closet." She said, as she climbed out of bed.

"Don't be gone all night." Nasir told her.

"I won't."

I was quiet as I watched her move through her oversized master bedroom, and into her outrageous walk-in closet. She shut the door with a click, sat down and came back into focus.

"Now, what's up?"

Since I knew she didn't have a lot of time, I told her about the situation with Maddox, and how we were pretending to date to help his reputation. I knew Joya would keep the secret. She was married to a music industry heavy. She understood playing the game.

"I thought the pictures at that benefit and the relationship came outta nowhere, but when I saw y'all at the anniversary party, it looked like the real deal Holyfield to me. I mean, the chemistry, though. He couldn't keep his hands off of you - had you sitting all in his lap, kissing all over your neck. When you left the party, it was like you all couldn't get outta here fast enough."

"That was an act."

"Sure ain't look like no act to me."

"Busy kissed me tonight. Like, for real kissed me."

"This is the first time he's kissed you?"

"Yeah, Joy."

"Uhm, I would've thought he was tonguing you down from day one. The way he was looking at you, though. He had me ready to take Nasir to the bedroom."

"We do have chemistry."

"Yeah, you do. So, I'm guessing that the kiss was everything and now you're bugging. You stay too much in your own head, MeMe."

"I don't trust anybody more than I trust me. I don't like letting other people in my head."

"Or your heart."

"Agreed." I said resolutely. It was my truth, I wasn't going to deny it - especially not to Joya, who knew me too well to believe an obvious lie.

"Well, if you wanted somebody to tell you to jump on that D, and let Busy bang out, you would've called Clarke...or River. Since you called me, you must want the real."

96

"Plus, you're older than us. Your opinion isn't colored by a past, misplaced crush on Busy. You can be unbiased."

"Where are you crossed up? Did you not like the kiss? Liked it too much?"

I sighed heavily, because I was about to have to admit the truth to my "big" cousin, and in the process, admit the truth to myself. "I like everything Busy does to me. I like it when he hugs me, holds me, touches me, kisses me, and he gives me these foot massages. I'm walking around in a constant state of...arousal, every time we're together. But at the same time, I don't trust Busy."

"Name me one person that you do trust, MeMe."

"You."

"One *male* person." She paused. "Besides Uncle B. and Cairo."

"I trust Brandon Mayhew, and Nasir."

"But you will never be in a romantic relationship with either of them. At least you better not ever be in a romantic relationship with Nasir."

We both chuckled.

"Here's my advice, girl - be open to the possibilities. Even if they freak you out, try to be open to them. When I met Nasir, I didn't trust anybody, even myself. So, you're one step ahead of me, because at least you trust yourself. And I won't lie, Nasir did fumble my heart. He did mishandle me and it hurt like hell, but to get where we are right now in life, I would do it all over again."

"Yeah, you can say that, now, Joy. But when you were on your Jazmine Sullivan, and wanting to "bust the windows out his car," you were probably wishing that you had left Nasir exactly where you found him."

"You're right." She conceded. "But Busy isn't Nasir. There's no guarantee that he's gonna do the same stupid stuff Nasir did. Look, I don't know athletics like I know the music industry, but I do follow Busy's social media. I don't see him loved up with women on there. It's pretty tame, Mecca."

"His social media might be tame, but if his personal life was tame, he wouldn't need me to pretend to be his girlfriend to clean his shit up."

"So, do you just wanna argue? Cuz if so, I'm going back to bed. I've got a whole husband that I could be snuggled up against right now." She stood up and started to leave her walk-in closet.

"I'm not trying to argue, Joy. I'm just trying to...process."

"Busy wilded out when his grandmother died. I know something about people reacting poorly to the death of someone close to them, cuz Nasir smooth went down the rabbit hole when his best friend was killed. I don't think the mess that Busy went through with that Ainsley Neuberg hoe, is his general character. I think that was grief, and hurt and sadness. Stop making excuses to deny yourself that boy's attention. I know that's what it is Mecca, at least part of it. You know Dr. Marva said that some part of you gets a little thrill from having the self-discipline to deny yourself where other people would give in to their nature." She lowered her voice, and it was filled with love and concern. "Sometimes self-denial is a punishment. Don't take pride in punishing yourself. You don't deserve it. You deserve the attention of someone as kind, gorgeous, sexy, successful, protective and skilled at foot massages as Busy."

"Tell Mecca that Maddox Mayhew wants her ass, and come back to bed." I heard Nasir say. "The entire time y'all was over here, dude never took his eyes off you. He was definitely giving off proprietary vibes."

I smiled in spite of myself. "Thanks, Joy-Joy. Thanks, Nasir. Go back to bed. We'll talk when I get back from Kentucky."

I heard Joya's gasp. "You're going to Kentucky with him?"

98

"Yeah, tomorrow night. We're attending some type of season kick-off, training camp kick-off, back-to-school barbecue on Sunday."

"Back-to-school? You're crazy. How long are you gonna be in Kentucky?"

"I think we're coming back Monday."

"Have fun." She sang.

Mecca

8

The flight from Chicago to Londynville, Kentucky was short, especially when you considered the fact that we took a private jet. There was no check-in, no TSA, no baggage claim, no waiting at our gate. In a little more than an hour, Maddox and I were deboarding the plane and sliding into the backseat of a black Infiniti QX80.

On the plane ride, Maddox told me that he'd put what he referred to as "the house of shame" on the market after the Ainsley Neuberg situation. We were going to stay at his new place in the heart of the city, downtown Londynville.

When the driver brought the truck to a stop and I saw where we were, I got majorly excited. His place was a red brick, converted firehouse. The doors where fire engines used to race from the building had been transformed into an oversized picture window, with a large flower box in front. The door that led into the home was painted...wait for it, fire engine red.

"Busy." I said looking over at him in shock.

He tried his hardest to hide the smirk that was threatening to overtake his lips, but he was losing the battle. "What?"

"It's a firehouse. You didn't tell me it was a firehouse."

"It's not. It's just a house. Ain't no scantily clad firemen up in here, so your little firefighter fantasies aren't about to come true." He teased.

"This is gorgeous." I jumped out of the truck without waiting for Busy to open my door for me like I usually would. I walked around the side of his home, taking in the beautiful red brick. When he joined me on the side of the house, I spoke again. "This brick is amazing. I love Chicago brick, love it. But for this project, I do prefer the more uniformed look of a manufactured brick."

"What do you know about that?" He asked, looking at me strangely. "You spend your free time rehabbing homes or something?"

"You know my little cousins own a design business. I hang around their projects sometimes." I shrugged my shoulders. "Sometimes, I think about going back to school for design. Plus, you know I watch a lot of HGTV."

We both chuckled.

The driver appeared with our bags in tow. "Your bags, Mr. Mayhew."

"You wanna stand out here admiring the bricks, or do you want to see the inside?"

I smiled up at the beautiful man who owned the beautiful home. "I wanna see the inside."

I waited impatiently, bouncing on the balls of my feet with anticipation as he unlocked his front door, and entered the code into his alarm key-pad.

I really should've been embarrassed by how brand new I was acting. I mean, Bryan and Janaye Goode had shown my siblings and me the world. They'd exposed us to travel, culture, high society, and privilege, but Busy's house was something different. It was perfection. If somebody had given me his exact house with a blank footprint, I would've created the exact same space, or at least tried to.

I stayed mum while the driver set our bags in the middle of the floor, thanked Maddox and went on his way, leaving Maddox and me alone in the space standing right by the front door. I took in the open floor plan, the finishes, the furnishings, the exposed brick, the stunning ash wood floors, and I was in love.

I turned my gaze to my childhood neighbor, who was clearly now all grown up. "Would you marry me, so I can live in this house?"

He watched me silently, and I could tell that he was calculating his response. He was taking so long to reply, that I was about to let him know that I was only joking, when he finally spoke. "If I marry you, do I get to touch you the way I can't stop imagining touching you?"

101

It was my turn to contemplate and ponder my response. How to answer that question? Should I make a joke and bring some levity back to the conversation, or give him the answer that had immediately popped into my mind?

"Anytime you want, as long as you promise to make it worth it." *Why did you say that?* I asked myself the second after the words left my mouth.

Raising one eyebrow, he stared at me. His words were just above a whisper, like he was concerned that if he spoke too loudly, I would bolt, but I knew that was based on the expression that was probably on my face. "I can make it worth it."

Sighing, I ran my fingers through my hair, because I needed something to do with my hands.

"What are you thinking, Mecca?" His deep voice stirred something inside the depths of my stomach, summoning butterflies where there hadn't been any before.

I sighed, again and was honest. "I'm thinking that you think you wanna go there with me, but it's really not worth the effort."

The confusion he felt at my statement was obvious from the expression on his face. "What's not worth the effort? You?"

"Trying to pursue something with me."

"Why? You aren't interested?"

I couldn't help smiling, even through the screw-face I was giving him. "Have you looked in a mirror lately, Busy?"

He smiled back at the compliment.

"Of course I'm interested. You already know that."

"I thought you were, but this conversation is throwing me off." He shared.

"Sorry."

"Nah, don't be sorry. Talk to me."

I took another look around our surroundings. I didn't get how we went from joking around about the fabulousness of his place, to...this. "Busy, if I promise that we can circle back around to this later today, will you let me rock - at least until after I settle in and unpack my bag?"

He studied me for a few seconds. "Yeah, if you give me a kiss."

"Give you a kiss? Are you serious?"

"Yeah, I'm serious. Look Pudding, it's obvious that you've got something going on. I can respect that, and give you the space to work it out, but you aren't a delicate flower. You can handle me. Come handle me, girl."

He was right, I wasn't a delicate flower. "You're lucky I like kissing you." I told him, as I stepped closer.

He pulled my body to his. "I am lucky." He agreed, backing me up until my back was pressed against the front door, then covering my mouth with his.

Tingles surged through my entire body, like Busy had overloaded a circuit inside of me. *Yep, this confirms it*, I thought to myself as Busy's tongue took control. *I love kissing this man*.

His mouth was just like the rest of him, powerful and commanding. Plus he was greedy and demanding. He put his fingers in my hair, and I could barely concentrate on his tongue work, because his fingers were sending shockwaves from my scalp all through my body. I moaned in his mouth, and he deepened the kiss.

That was when the trouble started, because that was when Candie (which would be my vagina) decided to get involved. I wasn't like one of those heroines in a romance novel whose coochie jumped every time the hero's character entered the scene. I prided myself on keeping a tight leash on Candie. I liked control and discipline in every aspect of my life, and she was no exception. Except apparently where Busy was concerned, because she was tingling, throbbing and making her presence known.

Breaking the kiss, Busy whispered in my ear. "You don't even know how badly I wanna say some nasty shit to you right now, then do some nasty shit to you."

He didn't even know how much I wanted him to say some nasty shit to me, and do some nasty shit to me right then.

He continued, "I'mma let you rock, like you asked. But just so you know, I can't make any promises about how long I'mma be able to keep my hands to myself." He shook his head. "We will revisit what we touched on earlier."

I agreed, not really concentrating on his words, because my damp panties were distracting me. "Okay. uhm, give me the tour."

He grinned, gesturing around the open space. "Cool, this is the foyer, and the living room. Over there's the dining room and the kitchen. Come on." He led me through the spacious living room, where there was a makeshift wall. To the left of that, there was a short hallway. "Behind that wall is the family room, but down this hallway, there's a bathroom, my weight room, and a guest room."

"Is this the only guest room?"

"There's a guest room upstairs. Why?"

"Uhm, I would feel more comfortable if I weren't left alone on the lower level of your mini-mansion. I mean, do I have to fend for myself should somebody come through one of these picture windows looking to secure the *entire* bag? I'm a guest, Busy. I think if somebody comes up in here, they should at least have to defeat your big ass first, so I have time to come up with an escape plan."

He laughed uproariously. "You're wild as hell, Pudding. Let me take you upstairs. I can't have you being put in harm's way on my watch."

I followed him up a set of industrial looking iron stairs in the middle of the room. At the landing, he turned around, pinning me with his eyes while he teased me. "And just so you know, I'm totally wit' it if you wanna sneak in my room and take advantage of me. You know I'm weak for you, girl."

"I'll try to behave myself." I deadpanned.

He busted a left turn, so I followed him. He led me to a darkly furnished, but brightly lit bedroom. "The bedroom downstairs is nicer…"

"I won't care how nice the room is if I'm bleeding out in it, Busy."

"I never knew you were this dramatic, Pudding. When my grandmother was trying to play matchmaker, she never mentioned your annoying characteristics." He rolled my bag into the room behind him.

"Forget you. What are we doing tonight, anything?"

"Nope." He shook his head, eyeing me like he was trying to gauge my reaction. "Just me and you."

"Okay." I nodded easily. "So, you wanna help me pick out something to wear to this team bonding thingy you're taking me to tomorrow?" I looked up at him with humor in my eyes. "I mean, I gotta make you look good."

"You always make me look good, Mecca."

I chuckled. "You always say that, Busy."

"Because it's true. You're making me look so good, that I'm already starting to wonder how I'mma let you go when it's time."

I stared into his deep brown eyes. Busy was distractingly gorgeous, and self confident as hell. He had the kind of looks, and demeanor that could have you out here making a damn fool of yourself. It took a lot of concentration on my part not to let him see how much he affected me. "You thinking about trying to make me a more permanent fixture in your life, Busy?"

"Hell yeah, I am. Am I not being clear? Ever since I left your place last night, all I keep thinking is that if I had listened to my grandmother way back then, when she first started trying to get me to pay attention to you..."

I don't know what came over me, but at that moment I wanted to kiss him, to feel his lips against mine. I let my hands find the hem of the t-shirt he was wearing and tugged him towards me. He was amenable to it, coming closer to me, then wrapping me in his embrace and bringing his mouth down to mine, as I stood on my toes. He kissed me passionately, sucking my tongue, claiming my mouth as his own.

Candie thumped excitedly. *Relax, momma.* I told her telepathically. *We are not having sex with Busy. First of all, having sex before you determine the nature of the relationship is hustling backwards, and that is some shit that I do not do, and you know that. Secondly...*

"Mecca, where'd you go, Baby?" Busy asked, his warm breath by my ear, as he questioned me softly.

Silly me, I hadn't even realized that he'd broken the kiss. "Huh?"

Placing his hand on my chin, he gently tilted my head up, so that we were gazing at each other. "Where'd you go?"

I stood there blinking, positive that I looked like a big fool as I tried to figure out what words to say to appease him, because he looked genuinely concerned.

"No where." I lied poorly.

His head fell to the side, and he twisted his lips in a way that let me know exactly how much he wasn't buying what I was selling.

"Uh..."

"Talk to me."

I threw a hail Mary. "Aren't we gonna be late?"

"For what, Ma? Hanging out together on my couch? Talk to me."

"It's just a bad habit. A really bad habit."

"Letting your mind wander while you're kissing?"

"Letting my mind wander during all kinds of intimate situations. *All kinds*, Busy. Catch the emphasis."

"You let your mind wander during sex, Mecca? On purpose or is this some kind of medical condition?"

I wanted to laugh, because really, what the hell medical condition caused a reaction like mine? But the expression on his face was serious, so I matched his energy. "A therapist told me once that it's a defense mechanism, a way for me to maintain control."

"Self-discipline even in the harshest of circumstances. I mean, your body wants to let go, and give in, but to give in would mean you have to give up control."

"Why do you understand this?"

"B.S. in Psychology. Hale Williams University, class of 2011." He joked. "Besides, I'm an athlete, I know all about the pride that comes from self-denial and mental strength. Playing through strains, pulls and even breaks. Pushing your body to its limits - mentally compartmentalizing pain...or in your case, pleasure. That shit's not healthy."

"It's not." I agreed. "But it's a hard habit to break."

He focused his attention on a spot somewhere over my head. "It's a learned behavior. Anything learned can be unlearned."

"That's what they tell me." I mumbled.

His eyes found mine, again. "It's true. It just takes time and a willingness to change. That's the problem with athletes, if we think a habit serves us well, even if it's unhealthy, it's hard for us to drop it."

"Don't be analyzing me." I teased.

"I'm not. I'm empathizing with you, cuz I do the same shit. Not where sex is concerned. I totally let myself go during sex. I feel *all* the feels."

He was grinning at me, and I couldn't help grinning back. He was just too damn fine.

"At least you can relate, other dudes...not so much. My last guy kept insisting that I didn't like sex." I pinned Maddox with my gaze. "I like sex."

"Maybe you just didn't like it with him."

I shrugged my shoulders. "Maybe. The bottom line is that in order for me to *give up control*, I would have to trust completely, and the only person I trust like that...is me."

"Okay. Okay. So, I'm guessing when you get intimate with yourself, you stay engaged."

I laughed out loud. "Definitely."

"I'mma put this out there, and you can do what you want with it - I have never backed down from a challenge."

"Did I challenge you? I don't remember challenging you. We were sharing, Boo. That wasn't me throwing down the gauntlet. That wasn't a challenge."

"Just keeping my hands to myself when you're around is a challenge, Pudding."

"Ugh, you're so corny, Busy."

He moved closer to me, even though we were only about a foot away from each other. "Let me off the leash, Pudding. Let me pursue you, date you for real. The shit that happened with them other dudes has to be unsatisfying. I'll help you relieve your frustration."

Ooh, he was so right. I liked sex, but it did have the tendency to be unsatisfying. Looking at Maddox, I didn't think there was any way that sex with him would be a flop, still, I wasn't going to tell him that. "Yeah, yeah. Every dude thinks he has the magic stick. But when we're in the middle of doing that thang, and I'm mentally planning my outfit for the next day, what then? You gonna want a do-over?"

"Oh, you're talking so much shit."

"You gonna make me eat my words?" *Please promise to make me eat words, then come through and actually make me eat my words.*

"If we're in the middle of doing that thing, and you're planning out clothes to wear…" he started.

I waited to hear whatever platitude he was going to spout about how hard he would make me cum, and how he would "snatch my soul," and all the other bullshit promises men liked to make.

"I'mma be highly disappointed in myself." He continued. "And you might hear me crying in the shower."

I screamed in laughter. "Wow. I can't believe you."

"And yeah, I might want a do-over." He chuckled.

I stared at him, imagining what it would feel like to let myself fall with Busy. To trust that this gorgeous motherfucker would actually catch me, and give me the same energy back. *A girl can dream.* I thought to myself.

He surprised me by pulling me to him and kissing my lips. "This is me, shooting my shot. Can I pursue you? I think it's fucked up that your last guy was too selfish to take care of you. I mean, it's obvious to me that you didn't give 'im your heart, but you did give him your body, and he couldn't even take care of that. I can see why you kept your heart to yourself. I'm not gonna even mention your heart, cuz you seem like the type to keep it under lock and key. But if you give me your body…I'll take care of it. Let me pursue you, Ma. Let me date you for real."

I didn't trust myself to speak, not completely sure if my mouth would say, "hell yeah!" or "Busy, that's not a good idea," so I just nodded my head.

He raised his eyebrows. "Yeah?"

I nodded again and I would've sworn that Candie was in my panties doing a "happy dance."

"Bet that."

Maddox

9

She agreed to me pursuing her. That shit was crazy, and I halfway didn't expect her to agree to it. Mecca wasn't necessarily easy to read, but she was candid. She wasn't one of those women who spent time trying to make you guess what she was thinking or feeling, she just told you flat out. I liked that shit. I liked a lot of shit about her. I had since the first day I hung out with her, when I took her to my youth camp practice, and she had my kids running plays with her.

She was beautiful, smart, witty, sexy, and some dumb ass motherfucker had slept on her, leaving her free and open for me to pursue. I didn't want to spend a lot of time on it, but dude must've been wack as hell.

Mecca wasn't an actress, she wasn't one of those chicks who pretended to be into the romantic/physical stuff to save a dude's ego. It was mad obvious when she checked out of that kiss. Her entire energy changed. Who the hell didn't notice something like that? The only thing I could figure was that the pussy was so good, he was too caught up to realize that his girl's head was on the other side of town while he was in it, working up a lackluster ass sweat.

Fuck him. I was up next, and there was no way in hell that I was gonna make the same mistakes he made. That was what I was thinking as we sat side by side on the couch in my family room later that night. Mecca was in soft pink - some type of cute, girly cropped top, and matching shorts. She looked pretty as hell with that soft pink against her honey colored skin. She looked like she held the key to my happiness.

Her feet were in my lap, and I was rubbing them while we half watched some movie with Kevin Hart on cable. I was in basketball shorts and socks. It was a calculated move, me not wearing a shirt. I wanted Mecca's mind on my physicality. If she was already thinking thoughts of a sexual nature, it would make it that much easier for me to keep her attention when I decided to love up on her.

"Busy, it's been a long day." She said.

"Let's call it a night, then." I suggested, gently removing her legs from my lap.

I stood up from the couch, and she stood up after me, yawning, and stretching her body in a way that was sensual without even trying to be. I stood there, glued to the spot watching the effortless movement of her body. Even her yawns and stretches had rhythm. How the hell did that happen? My dick jumped in my basketball shorts.

"Ay, come here, Mecca." I said, beckoning to her with my head, even though she only stood mere inches away from me.

She closed the distance between us. I didn't touch her, although I wanted to. I wanted to establish the ground rules, and I didn't want her mind, or my mind clouded while we talked.

"I need to touch you. Like, I have to touch you. And I'mma touch you everywhere that I want to touch you, in every way that I want to touch you, but if you don't like something I'm doing, just let me know. I'll stop, and try something else."

"Okay." Her voice was soft, but assured.

"I'm not gonna try to have sex with you, though. This ain't about that. This is about establishing muscle memory. I want to get to the place where your body recognizes and trusts that my body will provide pleasure."

She blinked a few times. "Well damn, Busy. That's sexy as hell."

I grinned down at her, nodding my head. "I need you to trust me, but I can't demand you to trust me in your heart on day one. That kind of trust is built over time. So, instead of that kind of trust, I'mma work on getting your mind and body to trust me to give it pleasure, and respond accordingly." I took a beat. "Is it okay for me to touch you?"

"Yeah."

"Oh, and if I see you floating off into space, I'mma call you on it. Don't leave me alone in this, Mecca. Do your part. Stay engaged. And I'mma do my part. I won't be so into the pleasure you're giving me that I get selfish and leave you out there by yourself."

"Okay." She practically whispered.

I guess she recognized that I was about to make things very real, because she went from assured to tentative. I was cool with that, though. I knew what I wanted to do, had been thinking about it for weeks.

I ran my hands over her arms, and felt goose bumps pop up at my touch. I didn't acknowledge them, instead, I ran my hands over her arms again, letting her get used to

112

the feel of my hands on her bare skin, the weight of my hands on her arms. Bending my head, I found the crook of her neck, and buried my face there, inhaling her scent. Mecca smelled delicious, like butter pecan ice cream - sweet, and buttery. Her scent brought to mind memories of summertime, sunshine, and laughter. I couldn't help sucking her there to see if she tasted as good as she smelled. When I discovered that she did taste as good as she smelled, I couldn't help sucking her there again, as my hands traveled from her arms to her back, rubbing her soothingly.

She draped her arms around my neck, seeming to melt into me like she had so many times before and I pulled us closer, pressing against her until her breasts were flat against my chest, and my hands were in her hair.

"You smell like ice cream." I told her, between nips and sucks.

She moaned incoherently.

"Tell me what you like, Mecca." I said, while my hands traveled her body, my fingertips and sometimes even my fingernails gently moving across her bare skin. After I touched everything, I stuck my hands back into her hair, resting my fingertips against her scalp, periodically tugging at random locks.

"What your hands are doing, what you're doing to my neck." She breathed.

"Yeah? What about this?" I moved one hand from her hair, and rubbed my right thumb across her left nipple. Even though I asked, I already knew she liked it, because her nipples were swollen to hard peaks before I even touched them. Slowly over her perfect mound, my thumb teased and tantalized, and even though I loved the way her arousal felt under my finger, I held myself in check. It wasn't about how I felt, it was about how she felt. I took my mouth off of her neck, and moved it to her nipple, replacing my thumb, covering her nipple through the fabric of her top. My hands moved down to her ass, cupping handfuls, dragging her up to her tip-toes.

113

"Everything about you is good, Mecca." I said into her chest.

She didn't respond, so I lightly circled her nipple with my tongue. Her hands left my neck, and involuntarily went into my hair. I liked the reaction, so I licked her nipple again, and followed that with a pulling suck. My right hand left her ass, and moved up her back until I came to the back of her bra. Quickly unclasping it, I pushed up her top and bra, then attached my mouth to her bare breast. I felt her knees slightly buckle, when I nipped her there. With hands as determined as heat seeking missiles, I found the top of her shorts. Sliding inside her panties elicited a vibration from low in Mecca's throat. That sound did something to me - caused my dick to go from semi-hard to completely bricked up in mere seconds. Mecca's pussy was bare. I was a sucker for a hairless pussy. When my hand made contact with her skin, I looked down at her and our eyes met.

She didn't say anything, but her eyes and her grin clearly communicated, *"Yeah, that's right."*

I couldn't help chuckling. "You got me." I admitted. "I definitely like that. But don't start celebrating, stay right here with me."

She nodded her agreement, but her energy had already switched, so I pulled my hands out of her panties and hugged her to my body.

"What?"

"You know what." I told her.

"I'm sorry." She apologized, looking remorseful.

"You ain't gotta apologize. You were right there with me for a while. What happened? When I touched your pussy you got nervous? Decided to pull back? Cuz you could've let me make my little discovery and keep going."

"I know."

"You know it's a choice to stay engaged, right?"

114

"I know."

"As long as you know." I told her with a shrug of my shoulders.

"You giving up on me?" She tried to keep her expression blank, but her eyes were too revealing. She was concerned.

"Hell nah." I leaned in and kissed her lips. "We're just getting started, Ma." I took her by the hand. "It's been a long day, let's head upstairs."

I left Mecca in the guest bedroom, and headed for the master. Once inside my room, I spent a minute gathering up things to pack for training camp. I was an organized person like that. It probably came from having so much chaos in my life as a shorty.

Once my mother got really sick, and everything was left to my dad to handle, shit just started slipping through the cracks. The first thing to go was household upkeep. Our house was my mom's showplace. She kept it clean and orderly, "a place for everything and everything in its place" was her life motto. Moms was a neat freak - probably borderline OCD. My dad loved that about her, he was always hugging her up and telling her how she took such good care of her four guys.

When she got ill, it was obvious that he didn't have the same predisposition to cleanliness that she had. It didn't take long for our house to fall into despair. Dishes piled up in the kitchen, clothes piled up in the laundry room, dust piled up on my mom's decorative knick-knacks. Shit just went straight left in a matter of weeks. Somebody had to step up, it was obvious that my mother couldn't do it, and my father wouldn't do it. Xavier was two and a half, he couldn't do it. That left Brandon and me. At seven and ten years old respectively, we became full-time students, part-time housekeepers and fill-in nannies.

In all honesty, I don't know where my father was or what he was doing while my mother fought the most harrowing and hopeless part of her illness. I just remember not really seeing him at home. I remember getting up every morning, showering and dressing myself for school, then waiting for Brandon to do the same. Next, I would get Xavier clean, fed and dressed, then put him in his stroller. The three of us would walk to Xavier's daycare, then Brandon and I would head to school.

You couldn't do that now. Somebody would definitely report my father to DCFS if he pulled some stuff like that in this day and age - having his ten year old drop off and pick up his 2 and a half year old brother from daycare. But back then...nobody said a word. Nobody cared, as long as my father paid, and that was the one thing he managed to do...pay. He kept the lights and gas on. Kept a roof over our heads, picked up groceries, paid my football, paid Xavier's daycare, and Brandon's computer class, but he damn sure didn't pay attention, or check in to see how his sons were handling watching their mother waste away. So, I checked in with Brandon. Used my fifth grade knowledge to help him with his second grade homework, laid out clothes for him, made sure he ate and showered and just tried to be a "good" big brother.

Things went from bad to worse after my mother passed away. The strand (as precarious as it was) that was holding my father together snapped, and the bottom fell out. But I guess he realized that he was ill-equipped to continue to front like he was handling things. He sat Brandon and me down, and told us that we were going to stay with our grandmother - his mother, until things "settled down."

Less than six months later, he enlisted in the Marines and never looked back. The irony of him enlisting in the military wasn't lost on me, even as a ten year old. His way of dealing with being too cowardly to face his wife's death and raise his sons was to do something that on the outside seemed very brave. I couldn't honor the shit. There was nothing brave about bouncing out on three vulnerable, scared, motherless little boys...even if it was to go to Iraq or Kuwait or wherever the hell he ended up. The war he needed to fight was right in his own heart and mind, not somewhere in the Middle East.

Personally, I thought the nigga had a death wish...he was trying to join my mother up there in heaven, so he didn't have to face the pain of losing her down on earth. He had a death wish, right up until he didn't...when he met Tiffany. Married Tiffany. Had three more kids with Tiffany. Kept it pushing with Tiffany and never looked back for my brothers and me.

I mean, he showed up at my NFL draft party in grandma's backyard with his new family in tow. That was an awkward as fuck encounter that I tried never to think about. He tried it again when Brandon got his law degree. My grandmother invited him to the graduation and to his credit, he showed, but again, we didn't know him...or his new family. So again, it was awkward. But apparently, the military gave him a "never give up - can do" spirit, because he was front and center again when Xavier was drafted and grandma threw that backyard turn-up a second time. That was less awkward, more stilted, because again, we didn't know him.

Whatever. My childhood left an impression on me, and part of that impression was to be neat, clean, orderly and prepared. So, I spent about an hour packing and arranging one of my suitcases. When I was finished, I headed downstairs to make sure all of the lights were off, check the alarm system, and handle whatever else needed handling before I laid it down. As I passed the guest room, I noticed that the door was open, and the lamp was on. I made my way down the hallway and stood in the doorway of the bedroom. Mecca was curled up in the middle of the bed, messing around on her iPad. She'd changed out of the shorts and matching top, and was in what looked like a sleep t-shirt.

"You cool?" I asked her.

She looked up, giving me a small grin. "Yeah. I'm one of those people who has a hard time falling asleep in someplace unfamiliar. I think it comes from traveling so much as a child. Sometimes we fell asleep in one country, and woke up in a whole different one. I might be a little traumatized."

She was traumatized? She didn't know the half. "Trauma comes in all forms."

She nodded. "Why're you still up?" She looked down at the screen of her device to check the time. "It's after one."

I shrugged. "I'm one of those people who has a hard time falling asleep unless I'm completely exhausted. If I try to sleep before I'm exhausted, a mental "to-do" checklist runs through my head on a loop, and I lay in bed watching the hours on the clock tick by, knowing I'm getting that much less sleep. I try to avoid that kind of stress, if possible." I took a beat. "You got enough blankets and stuff? You comfortable?"

"Yeah." She said, then narrowed her honey colored eyes at me. "You headed to the refrigerator? You up sneaking late night snacks, Busy?"

I grinned at her. "Nah. I'm about to check the alarm. I can't have nobody coming up in here trying to secure *the entire bag* and killing you in the process."

"Right." She agreed, and stood up from the bed, shoving her feet into colorful flip flops. "Come on."

I cocked my head to the side. "You coming with me?"

"There's safety in numbers." She said, like that explained everything.

It was whatever to me, so the two of us walked downstairs together. I checked the alarm panel, making sure to set every alarm. I probably wasn't always as diligent as I could have been, but with Mecca in my house, in my care, I took the extra precaution. She stood in the middle of my living room, repeatedly lifting her right leg while pointing and flexing her toes. For a few seconds, I was mesmerized by the definition in her leg, the way her calf muscle tightened, the way her quad muscle tightened. Just watching her was making me feel a way.

"What're you thinking?" I asked her, because her face was so focused.

She looked over at me, with a small smile on her face like she'd forgotten that she wasn't alone in the room. "That I could do so many pirouettes, fouettes and grand jetes in this one room." She admitted.

"Those are dance moves, right?"

She nodded.

I held out my hand. "Do ya thing."

"For real?" She eyed me.

"For real. Show it to me."

She looked around tentatively, and finally chose a spot that was decidedly open and clear of obstacles. She slipped out of her flip flops, kicking them off to the side. I watched as she centered herself, opened her arms, positioned her right leg and went into a series of quick turns right in front of me. It was wild, unexpected, and artistic, but also very, very sexy and beautiful. I stared in awe as she slowed, and stopped herself on a dime, the right leg that she started with, ending behind her.

"Damn." I said appreciatively. "How much dance training have you had?"

She kicked her leg into the sky, absent-mindedly flexing it, oblivious to the fact that my dick jumped at the movement.

"Probably since before you started in Pop Warner." She smirked.

"I was six when I started playing Pop Warner football."

"I started dance when I was three."

"Looks good on you."

"Thanks."

"So, you ready to head back upstairs, or you got some more jumps and turns that you need to get out?" I teased.

"I'm good. Cuz if I marry you, and move in here, I can do jumps and turns in this living room anytime I want."

It was weird that the fact that she kept joking about marrying me didn't freak me out. It actually had me bugging the opposite way, like I felt a sense of calm both times she said it, because at least that part of my life would be settled. I would know who and what I was coming home to when I got off the road. I would probably like coming home to a woman like Mecca, who was easy and laid-back and gorgeous and sexy as shit. Plus, she grew up with an industry father who traveled all of the time. She understood the lifestyle, and wasn't likely to be all insecure or in her feelings every time some chick posted a crazy picture on social media or something.

Why are you making up reasons to marry Mecca? I asked myself. *She's playing with you, and you're over here mentally wifing her and making a home.*

"Yeah, you can." I assured her. "As long as you do them naked."

"Whatever, Busy."

I stood back, and let her head up the stairs ahead of me watching every swish of her hips as she walked. I followed her to the doorway of the guest bedroom. She sat down on the bed and faced me.

"Uh, this is your house, Busy. You know you're welcome to come in here. You don't have to stand in the doorway."

I shook my head. "Nah, it's not like that, because whether this is my house or not, you're a guest. I'm not trying to infringe on your personal space. While you're here, this…" I gestured to the room, "is your space."

"Okay." She said with a nod.

"You're still not sleepy?"

"Nah." She told me. "And I feel like I should be, because I've been up for almost 24 hours straight, but I can't get my mind to shut down, yet. So, I'm watching this movie."

"On your iPad?"

"I always watch movies on my iPad." She shrugged her shoulders.

"You know I have a whole 75 inch t.v. in my bedroom."

"You trying to get me in your bed, Maddox Mayhew?"

With a shrug of my shoulders, I chuckled at her question. "I'm just offering you the opportunity to watch your movie on a larger screen."

She watched me for what felt like the longest seconds on earth. "If I lay in your bed and watch this movie, are you gonna keep your hands to yourself?"

I didn't even have to think about it. "Hell nah. If you get in my bed, Mecca, I'mma be all over you, but I will honor what I told you earlier. My end game won't be having sex with you."

"Your end game is helping me to stay engaged, while you're loving up on me, right?"

I nodded.

She stood up. "Let's go."

This girl.

I led Mecca into my bedroom. The two of us stopped at the foot of my bed.

"Which side do you sleep on, Busy?" She questioned.

"Right." I said walking over to the right side of the bed, sliding out of my slippers and sitting on the bed.

She walked over to the left side of the bed, and sat down.

"So, should I turn on the t.v.?"

"You don't have to, but could you turn on some music?"

"Yep, if you want music, we can do that." I grabbed my phone off the nightstand, did the whole "face recognition" thing and handed it to her.

She messed around on it for a little bit, handing it back to me when Earth, Wind & Fire's "Would You Mind" started floating from the phone. I stuck it in the phone dock, and the song filled the room through the speakers.

"Is this your little sexy playlist?" I teased. "You about to seduce me, Pudding?"

She grinned her pretty grin at me, batting her eyes a bit. "Maybe."

"Okay." I climbed all the way into the bed, scooted to the middle and pulled her into the bed with me. When she was on her back, I covered her upper body with mine, leaning into her as I gently kissed her lips once, then again. I trailed kisses from her lips, across her jaw line, and to her neck, while my hands swept down the sides of her, landing at her hips. I didn't know where her hands were, because they weren't on me. "Where you at, Ma? You in your head?"

"I'm not in my head." She assured me.

"I feel like you are, Sweetheart."

"Not in the way you think, Busy. You, and this music...I'm having a lot of sensations and I'm trying to process them."

"Mecca, don't process them, feel them. Stop fighting the flow. Cool?"

"Yeah." She heaved out, and then I felt her hands on my back.

I needed a minute to regroup, because shit, she was regressing. Now, she needed to "process" the sensations. I grabbed the bottom of her sleep shirt. "Take this off." I said pulling it up. She helped me take it off of her and I flung it into the darkness. "Make the decision to be in the moment, Li'l Mama." I must not have said it as gently as I meant to, because her face kind of fell.

"I'm sorry."

"Don't apologize." I said softly while caressing her cheek. "I'm about to level the fuck up. I need you right there with me...leveling up. We're about to figure out what you like, and what drives you wild. You good with that?"

"I'm not trying to be difficult."

I stuck my hand in her panties, swirled my fingers around her slick folds, pulled them out and showed them to her. "Your pussy's wet for me, Mecca. I know you're not trying to be difficult. I know you want this. Just decide to let me take you where you wanna go. Trust that I'm all about giving you pleasure." I whispered in her ear. "I got you, Baby."

I laid her back down, and this time I got between her legs, pushing them open with my knee, before I made myself comfortable there. I pulled her bottom lip into my mouth, and bit it softly, before soothing it with a gentle suck, then I plunged my tongue into her mouth, while simultaneously plunging my hands into her hair and pulling from her scalp. I tangled my tongue with hers, teasing her and tasting the flavor of Mecca. Even with her tendency to disengage, she was addictive, driving me to want to be the one who cracked the code to her satisfaction. I tugged roughly on her hair, my tongue doing the opposite, moving slowly and languidly in her mouth. Guttural sounds escaped from her throat and traveled into my mouth. I deepened the kiss, and ground my pelvis into hers, which I knew I was gonna regret, because that type of thing would cause me to get hard before I wanted to, but I couldn't help it. She was responding and that had me wanting to keep her responding.

I broke the kiss, and moved casually down her body, stopping at various points to place open-mouth kisses.

"Where are you most sensitive, Mecca?" I asked between kisses.

"My vagina." She moaned.

"Not yet, where else?"

"Right now? Everywhere."

I reluctantly removed my hands from her hair, because it was clear that her scalp was an erogenous zone for her, and I palmed her breasts. As a dancer, Mecca had a smallish frame, but her breasts didn't get the memo, they were a large C cup or a small D. They fit into my hands perfectly. I fed the right one to myself, sliding my tongue around her pretty mocha colored areola, while being inundated with that sweet, buttery smell that was uniquely Mecca. While I orally caressed her right nipple, I rolled the left one between my fingers, pulling and pinching periodically.

"Mecca, how do you feel?"

"Good." She sighed, her fingers were buried in my hair, holding me at her breast.

I gently nipped at her nipple, relishing its taunt peak, rolling it around in my mouth. I released her, and made my way south. When I was between her thighs, I kissed the inside of the right one, then alternately sucked and bit the same spot I'd kissed. I stayed there, repeating the sucking and biting, until I was sure that there would be a mark there for her to discover the next day.

"Aaaaahhhhhh." She moaned softly.

I moved to the inside of her left thigh, searching for where I wanted to leave her a reminder of our shared passion on that side. When I found a spot, I sucked and bit her there, too. While I worked on leaving a second mark, I slid her panties to the side, inhaling deeply so I could familiarize myself with the scent of Mecca's arousal. Deftly, I slid a finger inside of her.

She pulled in a sharp breath, treating me to a sweet hissing sound. I added another finger, while I sucked harder at the flesh on her inner thigh. As I pulled away from her thigh, I caught sight of my fingers buried inside of her. I'd promised myself that I wasn't going to bother her vagina tonight, but my mouth involuntarily watered at the sight and smell of her. She was grinding against my fingers, as they worked her into a frenzy so I decided to let her rock and save oral for another day.

I climbed back up her body, my fingers still working inside her core.

"You're gorgeous, Mecca. You're so fucking beautiful, Baby. You should come for me. You should let me see you come." I told her, before I swept her left breast into my mouth, and sucked desperately on her nipple.

I could feel the vibrations building in her body. I could literally feel them. I released her breast, so that I could look in her face when she came. Her eyes were squeezed tight, like she was concentrating with all of her might. She looked adorable, and mad focused at the same time. A few seconds later, her mouth flew open, and her facial features relaxed, but her eyes remained closed as she rode the waves, her body shuddering while she moaned loudly.

"*Damn, girl.*" I mouthed inaudibly, my dick jumping in anticipation as I watched her experience orgasm.

Slowly she peeled open her eyes. Slowly I removed my fingers from her vagina and placed them in my mouth savoring them, while she watched me intently.

"You taste good as hell." I told her.

"You feel good as hell." She responded.

I cocked an eyebrow. "Oh yeah?"

"Yeah." She nodded. Her breathing was starting to return to normal. "You're a really good tutor."

"Well, in my professional opinion, I feel like with enough extra credit, you could make the Honor Roll, Pudding. You're gonna need a lot of extra help, though." I paused dramatically. "I'm talking...a lot."

She grinned for me. "I think you're right, Busy. But first I need sleep. I'm gonna go back to the guest room."

I didn't want her to go, but I wanted to give her space. "Okay, Sweetheart."

She didn't move one muscle. I chuckled to myself, gathered her close to me, and rested my head on the pillow next to hers expecting to let my thoughts have free rein in my mind for a while. Surprisingly though, sleep pulled me under.

Mecca

<u>10</u>

I'd woken up in Busy's bed about six or seven hours after I'd fallen asleep. We weren't tangled up with each other, he was on one side of the large bed and I was on the other. I figured that was a tell-tale sign that we were both single and used to sleeping alone. The blankets were halfway off of Busy's body, so I could see that he still had on his basketball shorts. I was wearing panties, but nothing else. I did remember him taking off my sleep shirt, and tossing it into the abyss. I climbed out of his bed, retrieved my top, and quickly pulled it over my head.

I wasn't embarrassed about what went down between us, so I saw no reason to sneak out of his room like a one-night stand or something. Instead, I walked around to his side of the bed and shook him lightly. Without speaking, he reached out wrapping his arms around me and pulling me close. His hands landed on my ass, his face was pressed into my vagina.

"Good morning." He muttered.

"Are you talking to her or me?" I teased.

"Both."

"Good morning. What time do I need to be ready?"

"What time is it?"

"A little after 9:00."

He released me, rolling over onto his back. Busy had the best chest in the world. It was all of my favorite things...chocolatey, muscular and tatted up. It was like, a fantasy chest.

"We've got time. You hungry? I'll get up and make you something."

"I could eat." I admitted. "But first, I wanna shower. If you let me get clean, I'll help you whip something up."

"You cook, too, Pudding?"

I looked at him incredulously. "Busy, are you even serious right now? As much time as I spent hanging with Miss Vera and Auntie Bo - is there any way that you think I can't cook?"

"Well hell, if you learned from my grandmother, I'm about to let you do all the cooking."

I couldn't stop smiling to myself or looking down at my exposed thigh area as I stood in Busy's kitchen. I was cracking eggs into a bowl, separating the whites from the yolks.

"What's good, Pudding?" Busy asked me with a smile of his own. He was chopping fresh vegetables for the egg white omelet we were making. "You keep smiling."

"I know." I confessed. "You put hickies on the insides of my thighs at some point last night - this morning. Whenever." I told him, like he didn't already know that.

"And that has you over there giving me secret smiles and shit? Full disclosure, I'll put hickies all over your body if it'll get you to keep smiling at me like that."

"It was just like, a surprise. When I was putting on lotion after my shower, I was like, 'What are these marks?' then I remembered. I think it's kinda sexy. Like you and I are the only ones that know you were all between my legs...sucking on me." I gave him a flirty smirk.

He put the knife down and walked over to me, scooping me into his arms for a hug. "You can't say shit like that and not expect to get kissed." He covered my mouth with his, sweeping all logical thought from my mind.

Now that I knew that Busy had the patience and determination to make sure that he kept my body humming, my body seemed to hum for him automatically. Candie was throbbing and doing her best impression of a leaky faucet, my nipples were as hard as bullets, and my heart was thumping like crazy in my chest. I wasn't sure what was happening to me, but I didn't want to examine it, I just wanted to experience Busy.

"I'm trying to go slow with you, Pudding, but you aren't making that easy." He whispered into my neck after we broke the kiss. "You're sexier than a motherfucker, and I just...I just dig you. Plus you smell like ice cream, which has me wanting to eat you."

I caught the double entendre he was throwing. "Uhm. Is that why you were sampling my thighs? Because you wanna taste me?"

He looked down at me. "Yeah and I haven't had breakfast, yet. So, I'm hungrier than a motherfucker."

Next thing I knew, I was hoisted over his broad shoulder.

"Are you serious right now?" I asked, my head down by his ass.

He didn't respond, just kept it pushing to his final destination, which ended up being the first floor guest room. As he placed me in the middle of the bed, I admitted to myself that it was nicer than the room I insisted on sleeping in. Before I could even process another thought, Busy's hands were inside the waistband of the short-shorts I was wearing.

"Lift up." He instructed.

I lifted my hips, and he pulled them and my panties off of my body, throwing them to the floor. I'd barely registered the sensation of cool air hitting my bare vagina before my legs were pried open and Busy was tongue kissing my clit. My eyes immediately rolled to the back of my head at the sheer intensity of the pleasure he was creating in my core. Only one thought ran through my mind as I fought not to levitate off the bed, *"Damn, his mouth is juicy."*

I liked to have control of myself at all times, but my body wasn't waiting for instructions, it was doing its own thing. My hands made their way to Busy's head and tangled themselves in the kinks located there. My hips bucked off the bed and thrust my vagina further into his mouth. He responded in kind - by licking, sucking, biting and teasing me more thoroughly.

My toes curled into the plush mattress, as I acquiesced to the waves of bliss. My body hummed under the command of Busy's attention and my mouth followed suit, moaning and whimpering in delight. I felt like I was going to pass out, or like I was strapped to electrodes that were programmed to send shocks throughout my body at various levels of intensity in mind-numbing increments. Just when I was sure that I was about to lose consciousness, a surge of euphoria washed over me with a ferociousness I had never experienced. The moans felt like they started in my calves and tore from my throat so loudly that I felt like they shook the bedroom walls.

"You cool?" He climbed up my body and whispered in my ear.

"Sshhhh." I said, grinning as I placed a finger over my lips. "Let me float right here for a second."

"No problem." He agreed, matching my grin."I take it that you're enjoying having your life ruined. There's more where that came from."

"Word?" I asked, the grin never leaving my face.

"Yep. Told you I'm dedicated to keeping the "secret smiles" coming."

I watched from my vantage point on the bed as he took what looked like a three-pack of condoms from the pocket of his shorts, before divesting himself of them.

Busy's body was perfection. His broad shoulders gave way to a huge, muscular, almost granite-like chest. His torso tapered to cut, well-defined abs and a tight waistline. His thighs were thick and powerful, and his calves were capable and strong. But his dick...it was pretty. Chocolate, and hefty, and long, and fat. I could not stop staring at it, with one thought running through my mind as I eyed it. For all its mass, and girth, it looked...friendly. It looked like the type of dick that could be my life-long friend. My bestie, even.

"I need you naked, Pudding." He said, making eye contact with me.

Without my brain's consent, or even its participation in the decision, my body stood up from the bed, made its way over to Busy and dropped to its knees in front of him. I didn't really "come back to myself" until his dick was firmly secured in my mouth, destroying the back of my throat. I typically didn't give head-bangers. I'd given that up years prior, when I decided that if a dude wasn't pressed enough to give me his best and work to make me cum, he wouldn't get my best, either. So, I hung up my mouth-game.

Apparently though, it was much like riding a bike, because my mouth knew what to do. It was juicy as hell, slathering wetness along Busy's shaft, while I sucked with a jaw force that I didn't even realize that I had. My hands alternated between caressing his balls and sliding over the length of him, while I hummed contentedly. I glanced up at him only to catch him staring down at me. Our eyes locked. He dug his fingers into the messy bun that I'd assembled on top of my head before my shower, and pulled my head towards his pelvis as he moved his hips. Even as my eyes watered and I fought not to gag, I sucked harder, squeezed his balls more firmly, and pumped his dick more vigorously.

"Fuck, Pudding." He groaned, as he broke eye contact because his eyes were rolling back in his head.

I couldn't grin, because my mouth was full of him, but I was proud as hell of myself. While I was preoccupied with celebrating my own skill-set, Busy pulled his dick from my mouth with a plop.

"Get on the bed." There was no mistaking the level of bass in his voice when he spoke to me. He was ready to have me.

While he was protecting us, I pulled off my shirt, wiggled out of my bra more quickly than I ever had before and got in the bed on my back. Busy spread my thighs and was inside of me before I could even think. All I could do was offer up a sigh of contentment. I cradled him in my arms, as he plowed into me, slowly, deep-stroking me. I felt every inch of him in my chest, but he spaced the thrusts out enough for me to float in pleasure for a few seconds before the next mind-blowing stroke arrived.

Busy bit down on my shoulder as he pounded his pelvis into mine, the firm mattress providing resistance to the invasion. I lifted my hips and met every crash with a crash of my own, vocalizing my pleasure and digging my fingernails into the skin on his back. I tried to make thoughts as Busy and I connected, but my mind would only remind me of the sensations I was feeling. Tingles were happening in so many places; in my scalp, in my breasts, in my vagina. I couldn't even concentrate on every place that Busy had me feeling good. All I could do was moan his name, and throw the ass at him like he'd earned it, because of course, he did.

He brought his mouth to mine, kissing me deeply, his tongue easily finding mine and rubbing against it with passion. I could not get enough of him. I pushed my head up from the pillow to deepen the kiss, although I was sure there was no way to do that, because he was already kissing me like it was our last moment on earth. When we broke the kiss, he moved his mouth to my ear.

"What the hell are you doing to me, Mecca? You got me bugging on a whole 'nother level."

"Right back at you." I said, or thought I said. Honestly, I could've just thought it in my mind. I wasn't sure. I wasn't sure of anything, except that Busy was everything, and all I wanted was for the feelings he was creating to last forever. He was pulling my hair as he slammed into me, and I was practically hyperventilating from the sensations. I could feel the orgasm starting to build, and realized that I'd never been in this moment, experiencing pleasure so intense. It was my favorite moment. My favorite place on earth. Underneath Busy while he put in work.

Busy moved his hands under my ass, allowing himself to delve even deeper. Opening me up for him to experience unchartered territory and realms of Mecca that no one knew even existed. There was no way to keep myself from yelling out. From screaming out. From pushing my hips up towards him.

"I'm about to cum." I said through no volition of my own. I had never announced anything like that in my entire life.

"Good, Baby. Me, too."

And with that, he seemed to kick into overdrive. Within seconds the little thunderstorm that had started to build in my stomach turned into a full scale tornado and I was flying over the edge of self-control, experiencing the hardest orgasm ever and screaming at the top of my lungs about it. I was so out of it, I didn't even know what happened after I came. I glanced over and saw Busy lying right beside me with the cutest smile on his face.

"I think I passed out." I said, my eyes were heavy as hell, and I swear my body felt like jello, like there wasn't a bone or a muscle anywhere in there.

"What makes you think you passed out?"

"I don't remember anything that happened after I came." Frowning, I racked my brain for memories. "Did you come?"

"Fa'sho."

I was quiet for a few minutes. "Busy?"

"Yeah?"

"I'mma need you to run that back...see if you can make it happen again."

He cocked his head to the side. "You serious?"

"Uh yeah." I said, making my eyes big and nodding my head. "Did you miss the part where I said that the loving was so good that it made me pass out? I definitely need that again."

He watched me, finally deciding that I actually was serious. He rolled on top of me, and easily slid inside with very little effort. "Greedy ass." He muttered, stroking me deeply.

The sensation snatched my breath and made me moan involuntarily. Before I completely succumbed to the pleasure, I was able to voice one logical piece of important information.

"Condom, Busy." I groaned, as he thrusted into me.

"In a second." He said, lifting my thighs over his forearms and pushing my legs back so that much more of me was exposed to him.

He slammed into me like he was the quarterback, and I was his favorite receiver, because I caught every single pass. The first time we had sex was slow and sexy, this time the sex was fast and hard. The bed quaked underneath us as Busy pumped me with ferocity. I could barely catch my breath, let alone find the ability to match his tempo, because all I could think about was the pleasure in my core.

After I didn't know how many minutes of intense pleasure (because this time, I was positive that I was floating in and out of consciousness), I came shuddering uncontrollably, and yelling incoherent things loudly. As I allowed my head to fall back on the pillow, Busy pulled out of me and released his load on my stomach. He crashed down next to me, his breathing audible.

If I wasn't positive before, now I knew for sure that whoever I was messing with before Busy came into the picture didn't deserve me. I nodded off before I could even wipe him off of my stomach.

Busy took my hand and helped me from the truck when we arrived at the barbecue which was located at a mansion in a very upscale, gated community. He hugged me from behind and placed an open mouthed kiss on my neck, just as a uniformed maid (housekeeper, servant, worker - I don't know) greeted us at the front entrance (I won't say front door, because that's what I had, these people had an "entrance") and led us through the foyer.

We were intercepted by a pretty, peanut butter-colored older woman as we walked past the kitchen and were headed for a set of French doors that led to the backyard. She waved the uniformed woman away, and fixed us with a knowing smile. I figured the smile had something to do with the fact that Busy was still behind me, his arms still draped over my shoulders and he was periodically burying his nose in my neck, as we walked.

"I was wondering if you were even gonna make it, Busy." The woman said.

She immediately commanded my attention, because she referred to him as "Busy," as opposed to Maddox.

"Of course I was gonna make it." He replied easily. "I was just running a little late...because you know, there's not usually a specific start time for this event."

"Not usually." She agreed. "But Rob is one of the hosts this year, and he asked me to help out. You know how detail oriented I am."

"No one is more detail oriented than you, True." He agreed with a snicker.

"Which makes me the world's greatest mother, and the world's greatest agent." Her eyes challenged him to disagree with her.

He acceded with a nod of his head. "No doubt."

"There was definitely a start time, and you missed it by..." She glanced down at her gorgeous rose gold colored Audemars Piguet watch, "almost three hours."

"Your watch is beautiful." I said, no longer able to keep the thought to myself.

Her eyes bounced from the face of the watch up to my face, and she gave me a genuine smile. "You must be her. You must be Meeka."

"Mecca." Busy and I corrected at the same time.

She smiled again and cocked her head to the side. "I apologize, Mecca. I'm Ayana Truesdale, Maddox's agent. He likes to call me True, and you may call me that as well. It's nice to meet you."

"Thank you. It's nice to meet you, too." I said.

"Since I'm late, what did I miss?" Busy asked.

"Not much. Just the opportunity to show your girl off, and mix and mingle."

Frowning, Busy looked off over True's shoulder. "I don't need to show her off to none of these dudes." He disagreed.

"Uhm, this is new. " She said in a teasing tone.

"Fall back, True."

"Oh please, Busy. You know that is not about to happen. I wasn't sure I would ever get to see the day that Maddox Mayhew would be possessive about a woman." She glanced over at me with a look of appreciation. "Mecca, huh?"

I decided to get in on the teasing by giving her a big, dramatic wink.

"Oh, here y'all go." He said.

"Here you go." She corrected. "You're the one standing here acting so possessive that you don't even want to introduce your date to your teammates."

"I'm acting possessive because my date is gorgeous as fuck."

"Get out of my face, Busy Mayhew. I'll talk to you later." She rolled her eyes at him good-naturedly. "Mecca, it was a pleasure meeting you. I hope to see you again."

"Thank you." I said, as Busy took my hand and practically dragged me away.

The turn-up in the backyard was real. There were about 100 people milling around a huge space that included a grassy knoll, an olympic sized swimming pool surrounded by a huge deck, an outdoor kitchen, and an inviting patio covered by a large pergola.

There was a group of people chilling on the patio, I thought we would make a beeline for them, but nope. Busy led me to the outdoor kitchen, where he walked right up to the bar and ordered a drink for himself and one for me.

"You hungry?" I asked him. "I'll fix you a plate."

"Nah, I'm good." He looked around the backyard. "I don't wanna stay long."

"You brought me all the way to Kentucky for us to make a cameo?" I confirmed. It wouldn't make me a difference one way or the other. I was all about Busy, and was down for whatever he wanted. I just wanted him to be sure about what he was saying.

The bartender handed our drinks to him. He placed a glass of the signature cocktail, the Leopard-tini, in my hand and took a drink from his glass of Hennessy and coke.

"Nah." He sighed like he was annoyed. "I'm just not trying to have a repeat of the shit that happened at the benefit, but I guess I should show you off."

I giggled. "Don't think of it as "showing me off," Boo. Think of it as what it is...introducing me to people. To your teammates."

"Let's get this over with." He took my free hand in his, and led me around the backyard to meet his teammates and their women.

The last group of people we approached included Ayana Truesdale's son, Robeson Miller, Justus Alexander, Lance Gardner, his wife, Dominique, a guy named Emerick Jones, and his wife, Sheena.

"I see you brought my future girlfriend with you to Kentucky, Nigga." Robeson said, as soon as we walked up, a wide grin on his handsome face.

"What'd I tell you about that shit, Dude?" Busy asked him, but he was grinning as well, as he went in to dap Robeson up.

"Nothing. *She* told me that she was busy being yours, you just sat there like a sucker." He joked.

"But after she said that, what was really left to be said?" Justus instigated.

"Yeah, she's the first person in history to shut your ass up." Busy added.

Robeson just chuckled. "What's good, Beautiful?" He asked me.

I knew he was being disrespectful, but something about Robeson let me know that he was really just messing with Busy, and wasn't at all serious about getting with me.

"Hey. Reggie, right?" I narrowed my eyes and asked just to mess with him.

Busy laughed out loud.

"Ain't this some shit?" Robeson joked.

"I'm just kidding. How're you doing, Robeson?"

"Call me, Rob, Little Mama. I'm good. You're looking pretty, as usual."

"Thank you."

"For real, though. How did you end up with this burly, swoll motherfucker? Like for real. I've known him forever, so I know he ain't really got no game."

Busy shook his head. "I got enough."

I nodded in agreement. "He has plenty."

"Awww, you just gone break my heart, right here? In front of a crowd? No chill whatsoever?"

"You'll bounce back." I assured him. "You have a lot of personality. I'm sure there are any number of women just waiting for you to give them some energy."

He cocked his head to the side and watched me silently for a few beats. "You mighta just been bullshitting me, but that actually made me feel better about myself. I am somebody." He joked. He turned and looked over at Busy. "I like her, Dawg. She's good people."

"Hell yeah, she is." Busy responded, like that went without saying.

"She definitely has good taste in shoes." Dominique Gardner said, changing the subject.

I looked down at the Saint Laurent wedges, which were beautiful, but obscenely expensive, then looked at Dominique beaming at her. "Thanks, Girl."

I felt Busy slide my hand inside his. I looked up at him and smiled.

Mecca

11

About two days after the pictures from the Leopards' Season Kickoff Backyard Barbecue thingy hit the internet, social media was able to connect all of the dots that I was a professional choreographer, who also happened to be the eldest daughter of DJ B. Goode. All of a sudden, every blog was posting stories about us, and photographers were posted up everywhere they thought that either DJ B. Goode, Busy or I would show up.

My dad (of course) took all of the attention in stride. He stopped and posed for pictures, talked to whoever tried to talk to him, and basically turned every question or inquiry about me into a way to promote his upcoming projects. I loved that man. I also loved that Busy seemed to be following his exact same playbook. He never answered questions about me or made any comment that didn't put the spotlight back on him or his upcoming season.

Me, I basically stayed mum, and tried to remember to make sure that they always got my best angle when they photographed me. I didn't workout six days a week to keep my dancers' body tight for nothing.

Five days after leaving Kentucky, I was sitting on my yoga mat inside an Airbnb in Portland, Oregon. The Portland Pioneers Cheerleading team had brought me in to choreograph two routines for their upcoming season. My iPad was on the stand in front of me, while I performed a series of light stretches.

"So, you and Busy? I haven't talked to you, but I have seen how you two are blowing up social media." Joya said to me from where her face was displayed on the screen. "They seemed to catch quite a few shots of him loving you up at that barbecue. What was up with that?"

"That is a really good question." I deflected. "Because, we were only there for a little more than an hour, and I do not remember him being all that handsy."

"Looked like he was being handsy and lipsy." My cousin Kyndall said, her face coming into focus on the screen.

"Definitely lipsy." Joya agreed. "I mean, you could barely see his face, it was buried so deep in your neck, or in your shoulder, or in…"

"Her mouth?" Kyndall interjected.

Joya glanced over her shoulder at Kyndall. "Exactly."

"Well, let's just say that it was a good weekend." I said, reaching for my toes and elongating my back.

"A good weekend filled with good sex?" Kyndall questioned.

"Yeah, were you doing splits on that dick?" Joya joked.

I couldn't help laughing. "Oh, the visual, Joya. Nah, I wasn't doing splits on that dick." I'm a professional. I pretended to grumble, but in the back of my mind I was already thinking about how to incorporate some splits into the mix the next time Busy and I got down. "Let's just say that Busy is a skilled athlete, and he's very attentive to detail."

"Basically, you're turned out." Kyndall concluded.

"How did you manage to leave him in Kentucky? How are you not putting your condo on the market and relocating? I'm saying, even in the pictures, the chemistry is hella thick between you two."

My eyes widened. "We are not on that." I told Joy, shocked that she would even take it there. "I mean, we spent one weekend together. I don't care how crazy the chemistry is, I'm not about to fall into him like that."

"Famous last words." Kyndall said dryly.

"Whatever, Kyndall." I said dismissively.

Of all of my cousins, Kyndall and I were the most oil and water pairing. We didn't seem to mix. I could and tried to get along with everyone, particularly my cousins, because we'd been raised to believe that family was your foundation. The Watsons believed that you learned social skills, conflict resolution, citizenship, good sportsmanship, fairplay, loyalty, honesty, integrity, respect, tolerance and acceptance from family. We didn't bicker amongst each other, hate on each other, plot against each other, hold grudges against each other, and we definitely didn't fight each other. Still, Kyndall didn't really like me.

I'd tried for years to win her over. Once I accepted that she just wasn't going, I decided that I wasn't beat to kiss up to her, so I gave her back the same energy she gave me. If she came at me positively, she received positivity in return. When she showed her ass, she got my ass to kiss in return.

Joya knew what time it was with Kyndall and me. She'd tried to mediate enough "let's get to the bottom of this" bitch sessions between the two of us, that went nowhere because Kyndall was never able to or willing to voice her actual problem with me, or admit that she even had a problem with me. She changed the subject. "How was practice today?"

"It was cool. They learned both routines today. We'll drill them tomorrow, run them on Thursday then I'll be outta here."

"You headed home after that?"

I shook my head. "Nope. Dallas."

"When are you supposed to see Busy?" Joya asked, like she was concerned that I was neglecting him or something.

"When I leave Dallas. I'll probably fly into Kentucky and spend a few days with him before he has to head to training camp."

"You kinda have to, Little cous. I mean, you can't send that man off to training camp without tightening him up." She schooled.

"Isn't there a rumor amongst the cousins that you're sexually repressed? I don't understand where the hell it came from, because everytime I talk to you the conversation is dick this, sex that, throw that ass in a circle." I joked.

"I think Joya started that rumor herself." Kyndall chimed. "I mean, how the hell are you sexually repressed with four kids in five years and another one on the way?"

My jaw hit the floor. "Oh my word, heifer!!!! Are you pregnant, Joy??!!"

Her back was to the camera as she swatted at Kyndall. "That wasn't your secret to tell, Kyndall." She huffed. "And you accuse Mecca of having a big mouth."

My jaw hit the floor again. I had no idea that Kyndall was saying I had a big mouth behind my back.

Kyndall's face appeared in the camera. "That's inaccurate, Mecca. I do not say you have a big mouth. I say that you tell Auntie Bo all of our business. There is a difference." She clarified. "Besides, I've said that to your face plenty of times."

"Whatever, Yamp." Joya told her. "All I know is that you're the one who spilled the beans, not Mecca."

Both Kyndall and I howled with laughter at Joya calling her a "yamp."

"How pregnant are you, Joy?" I asked, once I regained my composure.

"About ten weeks." She admitted.

143

"Why didn't you tell me?" My feelings were hurt, because Joya truly was my closest cousin. I told her everything. If Kyndall hadn't been on FaceTime with us, I would've gone into explicit detail about my time spent in Kentucky.

"MeMe, you know I would've told you first. Nasir and I were keeping it to ourselves until I made it out of the first trimester. Kyndall was being nosy, and spotted the pregnancy app on my phone."

"You say nosy, I say inquisitive." Kyndall told her.

I chuckled at that. "It's late there, ladies. I won't hold you guys any longer. I'll talk to you when I get back in town. Congratulations, Joy. I can't wait to get home and rub on your belly."

Maddox

I picked Mecca up from the airport when she came back through Kentucky. I sat in the back of my Infiniti QX80 waiting for her to come out of the doors, and calm me with her presence. There were so many other things that I could've been doing. Training camp was less than a week away. There was stuff that needed to be handled before I went off the grid for four weeks. But I would rather sacrifice something falling through the cracks while I was at camp than forfeit the opportunity to spend time with Mecca.

I watched her come through the exit door. She had on a pair of skin tight, dark denim capris, a pink oversized cropped sweatshirt that hung off of one shoulder and showed her 6 pack, her signature high heeled sandals and pink and gold reflective sunglasses. It was

144

no wonder that the media had started snapping pictures of her like crazy, she looked like a fucking star. She looked important as hell...to more than just me. To me, she looked like the sunshine. My contentment. The smile on my face. To others, she just looked bad as fuck, and she was that, too. But to me, she was happiness.

Heavy jumped out of the truck, ran around and opened the door for her. She slid across the backseat, engulfing the vehicle in her signature scent, that to me smelled like butter pecan ice cream, but she told me was actually a combination of Sol de Janeiro's 4Play shower gel, Sol Cheirosa '62 perfume and Bum Bum cream.

Before we could greet each other, my mouth opened and I spoke. "I wanna marry you." I was shocked as shit at the words that had come from my mouth, but I didn't regret them.

"Wh...what?" She asked with an expression that was halfway between a smile and complete astonishment. "What?"

"I wanna marry you, Pudding. Not today or tomorrow. But at some point, I see that for us. Like, the next time I'm heading to training camp, I want you at my spot, going down my checklist with me making sure I have everything. When you come home from choreographing or teaching dance classes, I wanna pull your feet into my lap and rub them. When I finish up a long stint on the road, I wanna know that I'm coming home to you. I wanna give you orgasms that make you pass out for the foreseeable future. Like I'm digging you to the point that I'm bugging the fuck out about not being able to be with you when we're apart. Shit's ridiculous, but I can't pretend like I ain't feeling it. I don't even know how to handle the thoughts in my head."

She watched me silently and let me get everything I wanted to say out before she finally spoke.

"You can't just say stuff like that, Busy. When you start talking about future and...marriage and stuff, you gotta be serious. It can't just be because you missed me, or

145

you were a little lonely, or I have bomb coochie, Busy. I'm a woman, when you say stuff like that, my mind will start working and planning. I'll be running around putting the things you say that you *want* in motion, then you'll be off with your guys talking about "she's getting too serious." You probably need to sit with these feelings for a minute. Process them. Evaluate them."

She was speaking calmly, but her eyes were wild, and I knew exactly what time it was. The truck wasn't the place to have the conversation that we needed to have, so I sat back and chilled.

When we got to the house, she immediately disappeared into the powder room. I carried her bag upstairs and put it in the master bedroom. As I made my way down the stairs, I spotted her sitting on the sofa in my family room. I joined her there, taking her right foot in my hand and unfastening the buckle of the strappy sandal, so I could massage her foot.

"Mecca," I said softly. "I didn't mean to overwhelm you, Baby. I know you're skittish as hell, and trust is not your thing. That was not the way to come at you, but I gotta be honest - that was not like, a planned speech. I promise on everything. Those words slipped outta my mouth before I had time to consider them, so I definitely didn't have an opportunity to edit them. But the fact that I didn't plan to say those words doesn't make them any less true. And it ain't about loneliness, or missing you or bomb pussy...even though all three of those things might apply. It's about the way I feel when I'm with you. The way I feel when I'm not with you. What I see when I look at you, Mecca.

I'm 32 years old, Mamas. I'm a grown ass man, who's on grown ass man shit. I wouldn't waste your time - ask you to tie yourself down to me, just because I'm better with you than I am by myself. I need for me and my woman to be better together. I'm good by myself, Ma. I've done this NFL thing by myself for ten years. I could be completely cool finishing it out by myself. I've done this "single dude" thing even longer.

But I am better with you, Mecca. I'm a better Maddox with you. But I want you to be better with me, too. I want you to feel like you're a better Mecca with me, too. If you don't feel that way, then we don't need to go no further. Let's pump the brakes, finish out this "fake couple" assignment and go our separate ways."

She picked up my hand, and laced her fingers through mine. "Busy, I trust you. I trust you to be the man that Miss Vera raised you to be and that you've shown me you are. I just don't gamble with my heart. With my body? I'm a dancer, I take a lot of risks with my body. I'm even cool with gambling my money, but my heart? You know that's asking for a lot."

"I know." I admitted.

"But I wanna give you my heart, and I have never wanted to hand my heart over to a man in my entire life. It scares the hell out of me that I'm even considering giving it away." She took a deep breath. "Like, giving somebody the power to hurt me in a way that I've never been hurt before. That scares me to death."

"I know it does," I said, and honestly I knew it did. "I could tell by the look in your eyes when we were in the truck. You looked like you wanted to be anywhere, but there. If we weren't on the expressway, I feel like you might've tried to tuck and roll."

She laughed out loud. "I wouldn't have." She denied. "I *was* freaking out a little. Your words, though. You said that you wanna marry me."

"Not tomorrow, Pudding."

"I know, Busy. But I'm like, damaged goods. I don't trust. I don't let myself go during sex. Like, I'm messed up." She shook her head.

"Everybody is messed up. Hell, you think I'm not messed up? Your "flaws" don't diminish the feelings I have, or what I see when I look at you." I said, lifting her left foot into my lap, and fiddling with the buckle.

"What do you see when you look at me?"

"My future."

"Next year, when you're getting ready for training camp, I wanna be here helping you. And when I get home from choreographing and teaching dance classes, I want you to rub my feet. And I want all of that other stuff you said in the truck. But first of all, I want you to promise that you're gonna continue to be patient with me. I already know how dudes will do you. They'll tell you that everything is sweet when they want you, and as soon as they get you, what they thought was cute becomes annoying."

"I promise that if I start finding you annoying, we'll figure it out. We'll talk it out. I promise not to treat you like shit about it. Okay?"

"Okay." She agreed, rubbing her cheek against my chest. "Let's date with intention, because I'm already like, majorly in my feelings about you. I probably love you, but I'm not ready to cop to that."

"I'm in my feelings about you, too. I probably love you already, too."

"You're not ready to cop to it, either?" She asked.

"Nah, I'mma need like, at least ten more shots of ass before I can cop to that."

"Tuh." She balled up her fist.

148

I caught it before she could land her punch. "You're my baby, Mecca. Even though you're still being stingy with yours, my entire heart belongs to you."

She stared into my eyes, before wrapping her arms around my neck and leaning into my ear. "I love you, too, Maddox Mayhew."

The End

Afterword

I hope you enjoyed the story of Maddox "Busy" Mayhew and Mecca Goode. Please look out for my next book, scheduled for release December 2020.

For updates and more information, please visit me at:

Website: tracygraypresents.com

Facebook: facebook.com/authortracygray

Twitter: @alwaystracygray

Also, if you enjoyed this expression of my creativity, please consider leaving me a review at Amazon.com or Goodreads.

Thanks!

~ Tracy Gray

Made in the USA
Monee, IL
25 October 2020